GRIM FEVER

R Scott Mather

overmorrow press

This is a work of fiction. Names, characters, businesses, places, events, locales, and incidents are either the products of the author's imagination or used in a fictitious manner. Any resemblance to actual persons, living or dead, or actual events is purely coincidental.

Cover design by the author.
Handprint image by Artturi Mäntysaari.

rscottmather.com

Acknowledgments

My heart goes out to all those affected by the recent pandemic, whether directly from COVID-19, the loss of loved ones, stress, anxiety, depression, job loss, or any of the myriad challenges presented to us globally. Also, to all the healthcare workers—thank you for your dedication.

I want to thank Tom Celik, Louis Robinson, and S.L. Baron for their feedback on this book. Charlie Knight edited this book and provided suggestions and honesty that exceeded my expectations. I look forward to working with them again. And to my family, who allowed me to work *mostly* uninterrupted—thank you for your endless support and love.

To Jenny, Bryn, and Elliot.

Everything for you, always.

PART I

1

The fever came two days ago, kicking off a mosh pit inside my skull. Now, aches roar in every joint, every bone. The skin on my chest crawls but scratching only worsens it. With no sleep at all last night, it's unlikely I'll be able to doze this morning, so I peel off my damp sheets and fling my legs over the side of the mattress. I have to steady myself. Just sitting upright, my bed is a canoe caught between ocean swells.

I wipe my sweaty palms on my shirt, grab the remote from the nightstand, and turn on the TV. Spokane Saturday morning news. Text scrolls across the bottom of the screen: SVE-1 'Grim Fever' Virus Linked to Encephalitis Deaths. The studio reporter, a baby-faced man with his Windsor knot too tight, says, "The virus, believed to be responsible for over ten thousand deaths nationwide, has epidemiologists baffled. Known on social media and other corners of the internet as 'Grim Fever,' the virus spreads via skin contact. Symptoms typically appear within twenty-four hours, and to date, it has a one hundred percent mortality rate. Experts say development of a vaccine is unlikely because of the rapid mutation of the virus. In local news, outbreaks at the pr—"

I change the channel to ESPN for background noise more than anything. The virus is all anyone talks about, and I'm sick of hearing it. 'Grim Fever' sounds more like a horror movie.

Nature calls, so I shuffle to the bathroom, twinges in my legs and back slowing my pace. After relieving my morning bladder, I strip off my shirt and look in the mirror. The purple-red rash has blossomed from my chest up to my neck. Damn it.

I need to get moving, so I rally my achy bones into the shower. The faucet handle squeals as I turn it to the blue 'C,' then lather and rinse as quickly as my body allows. Cold showers suck, no matter how often I take them. It's something I've never been able to get used to.

I finish getting ready in impressive time despite a few dizzy spells, then grab my coffee tumbler and a breakfast bar and head to work. My supervisor lets me clock in for a few hours on weekends, even though I'm not on the schedule. "I can always use spare sets of eyes and hands," he always says. I think he just enjoys my delightful demeanor.

Corrections Officer never appeared on my career aptitude tests in high school. Spending all day surrounded by murderers, rapists, and child molesters isn't anyone's ideal gig, but it's perfect for my current situation. For example, I've been watching a serial kid toucher for the past week; he'll get some hands-on attention today.

I've been at Spokane Correctional Facility for six months. It's my third prison in almost two years. The prison in Montana was okay, but the job paid in 'thank yous' and loose change. Before that, the facility in Cleveland paid well, but management was strict and made things difficult with my...special needs. I'll miss it here. The pay is decent, and most of the other correctional officers are tolerable—with a few exceptions. But the number of inmates infected with Grim Fever is growing too fast, so my time here is nearing its end.

It's my fault, of course. The number of virus cases, that is. I've lived with the Grim for the past two years, give or take a month. I don't know how I got it, don't know why it hasn't killed me. What I do know is that this bastard disease flares up every four or five weeks; I know when it's time because my hands trickle sweat like a busted showerhead. And if I don't touch someone and infect them, the symptoms rage to the point of a living hell.

I drive into the employee parking lot. It's empty.

Tabitha stands in the attendee booth, head cocked and mouth knotted to the side. "Hey, Officer Chaucer. Can't let anyone in today. Didn't you get the alert?"

"No. What happened?"

"Locked down for quarantine. A bunch of inmates got that Grim Fever business."

Shit.

"Can I park and call my supervisor?"

"Sorry." She twists her lips and shrugs. "No one goes in. Orders are orders."

The steering wheel is glossy with sweat. I look at Tabitha and force a smile. How easy it would be to reach out and grab her hand, thank her for being cheerful every morning. To transmit the virus and allow it to absorb into her skin. It would buy me another month.

I shake my head.

Tabitha is kind. A single mother who works two jobs. I can't let my desperation cloud my judgment. She does not deserve this misery.

I grin. "Got it. Thanks. Be safe out here."

"I will. You, too." Her smile is welcoming and bright. I can't believe I considered passing this on to her. Sourness stings the back of my throat.

Now what? I've thought about moving to Denver. Maybe I'll find a charming penitentiary there. The prison here worked out for me, but I can't continue spreading the Grim. I've infected eight of humanity's worst, and it's a reasonable assumption that they transmitted it to others in the prison population. I should have asked Tabitha if she knew the number of infected inmates.

Damn it.

I head east with no destination. I have to focus. I need a new home. But before I make my relocation plans, I need to come up with Plan B for today. Where can I find someone who deserves this curse? I struggle to think of places where seedy types might hand out. Strip club? Maybe I'll find a meth dealer or an abusive twat looking for his next punching bag. I pull into a McDonald's parking lot and pull out my phone to Google the closest gentleman's club. As I type it out, I receive a text message:

```
To all prison staff, the facility is
under quarantine...
```

Timely.

I finish my search and discover that Pleasure Playground is only four miles north. I get back onto the street and head for my destination. After a couple minutes on the road, the edges of my vision go gray. My skin burns like I'm radioactive. I yearn for the euphoric release that comes when I pass on the virus. The instant shift from agony to ecstasy is a feeling unlike any drug could deliver. I'm an addict jonesing for another hit of relief.

I've tried letting the disease kill me. Several times. Laying in a hotel room bathtub, bathing in my sweat, waiting for my insides to sizzle and turn to a bubbly goo. But before I could succumb to the symptoms, it was like the virus seized control and forced me to spread it. An attempted overdose didn't work either. I puked up an entire bottle of pills seconds after ingesting them with the virus acting as my stomach's bouncer. It keeps me alive to keep itself alive.

I pull into the parking lot of Pleasure Playground. No cars. Damn it. Chad, you idiot, it's nine a.m.—no strip clubs are open this early. I'm losing focus.

Something taps my leg. Droplets fall from the steering wheel like a leaky spigot. My hands are soaked, and soon my pants will look like I had an unfortunate incident at a urinal. A fiery itch creeps up my neck. The rash is spreading. I have little time before the virus seizes control and forces me to cross a line.

I had a list of people for situations like this during my time in Montana. I called it my Rolodex of the Damned. I'd pay a visit to the next jerkoff on the list, touch him, then go on my way. But here, I haven't needed it. If the situation called for it, I'd go into work, my supervisor would assign me to a section, and I'd find the most ravenous convict to infect. I've become too reliant on the prison. I need to diversify.

My heart booms like a brick in a dryer. Thud-thump. Thud-thump. Faster. Harder. My eyes go blurry. I'm not going to make it much further, so I pull into a spot near the Starbucks in the corner of the lot. I want to run inside and grab the first person I see or touch the homeless man who just hid his bottle of vodka behind the bus bench. Anything to stop this agony.

Time won't allow me to be as picky as I'd like, but I have to try and hold myself to some sort of standard. But I might not have such luxury today. I swallow the knot in my throat and accept that I might have to choose someone who doesn't deserve to die.

I slide out of my truck, legs buckling under my weight as I land on the asphalt. I blow out a long exhale and steady myself against the truck's fender.

A man and woman walk past me, both white-haired and frail, skin speckled with time, holding each other's hands. They've both lived long lives. Would it matter if they died a year too early? The man waves and nods. The woman smiles, a streak of hot pink lipstick on her two front teeth.

No. Not them.

I suck in a breath and push myself off the truck. My feet clump like my shoes are made of granite. Once inside, I shove my hands in my pockets. Moisture seeps through the fabric on my thighs. The older couple stands in line, still holding hands. In the seating area, five teenagers huddle around laptops. A woman in a red tank top with straight black hair in a ponytail sits in a club chair. She thumb-taps her phone, running shorts riding high up her thighs. A man perpendicular to the woman peeks over his book, eyes fixed on her tan legs. I name him Peep in my mind.

Peep could be a promising target.

The seat next to him is open, so I shuffle over and plop into it, sure to crane my neck as if I'm looking for someone particular. Peep side-eyes me, then returns to his book. Or the woman. I can't tell from this angle. My throat sinks into my chest, sweat leaches from my pores. The virus is on the brink of exploding, and I need to make this happen now.

Peep is wearing a long-sleeved shirt. Not ideal, but at least his hands are exposed. I can stand, pretend to lose my balance, and grab him on my way to the ground. I only need a second of skin-to-skin contact. I try to convince myself that this guy is planning to do something worse than ogling her bare legs.

This guy is horrible. He has to be.

I push myself off the chair at the same time he stands up.

"There's my girl," he says. He steps around a small table, grabs a coffee cup I didn't realize belonged to him, and walks toward the entrance where a red-haired woman stands holding a baby dressed in pink. Peep kisses the baby's bald head, then kisses the woman on the lips. "I got you a flat white," he says to her.

Damn it.

The young family leaves.

Shit.

I slump back into the chair. The headache makes my eyes vibrate, and a current inside my stomach threatens a dry retch. Much longer, and I'll be forced to grab the next person within an arm's-length. My mind spins.

The elderly couple shuffles into the seating area, scanning for two chairs near each other. The woman in the red tank top looks up from her phone and stands. "Here, take my seat." She smiles and moves to the 'Pick up here' spot by the front counter. The old man gestures for his wife to sit, and he gingerly settles into the chair next to me. His liver-spotted hand sits atop the armrest, inches away.

I turn away and look out the window.

Damn it, Chad. Think! Where can I go?

When I was in Cleveland, I found my way into the ICU of a hospital. Sweat dripped off my fingertips as I searched for a terminal patient. I'll never forget Sandra Medina's face as she lay in her bed, peaceful, unknowing. I gripped her exposed leg above the ankle. The rush of relief overlaid any sense of guilt at the time, but that moment will haunt me forever. I still see her face.

Sandra reminded me of my Leanne—full lips, chubby cheeks, wavy brown hair. I rub my thumb on the finger that once bore my wedding ring. My chest aches like someone unplugged my heart, and it has nothing to do with the virus.

I shake away the memories. How close is the nearest hospital? I slip the phone out of my pocket, but I can't unlock it because my fingers are too wet for the touchscreen. I groan, wipe my hand on my jeans, then pull up a search. The nearest hospital is twenty-two miles from here. I huff through my nose. I don't have twenty-two miles in me. The virus has its claws dug in and won't relent until I share it with someone close. There has to be someone nearby who's gotten away with something horrific.

I get up to leave, and the white-haired man smiles. "You remind me of my grandson," he says.

On any other day, I'd joke with him, tell him something along the lines of, "Oh, you're too young to be my grandfather." Then I'd wink at his wife and say she was too young for him.

Instead, I strain a weak smile. "Have a good day."

Outside, people chatter on the patio. A car honks when a pickup truck doesn't move after the light turns to green. I stagger to the corner of the intersection with the hope I'll stumble across someone to poison with my curse. Drug dealers and pimps are working at this hour, right? Are there even pimps in Spokane? I scan the street for seedy back alleys, a mugger, anyone that can help me stop the orchestra of screams in my head.

The woman in the red tank top stops next to me at the crosswalk, one hand holding a venti iced something-or-other, the other thumbing on her phone.

A thunderous roar erupts to my left. A white Mustang accelerates to beat the light.

Bing. The crosswalk signal changes to the green silhouette of a person, but the car swerves into the turn lane and guns it.

The sleeve of my t-shirt rustles as the woman in the tank top moves forward. Her eyes focused on her phone, she takes a step into the crosswalk.

I grab her bare shoulders and yank her from the path of the speeding car. Her cup flings forward into the street, the phone slams onto the sidewalk.

The engine growls, and rubber squeals as the car escapes.

The woman stares glass-eyed at the tan puddle splattered on the street, a green straw propped up on an ice cube. She looks at me, mouth open. "Ohmygod. You saved my life."

If only.

A surge of electric energy gushes through my veins, and my head floats like a balloon tied to a string. Every ache in my body dissipates, the sweat on my hands vaporizes, and the crushing weight on my chest disappears. The virus has released its grasp, freeing me.

For another month, at least.

The woman stares at me. "My heart is racing right now. Oh my gosh. Thank you."

I pick up her phone and hand it to her.

"Thank you so much." She hugs me, presses her face into my chest.

What do I say? 'You're welcome, but you'll die in a week from Grim Fever?'

My mind is a mangled heap of emotion. Physically, I feel like a superhero.

But superheroes don't kill innocent people.

I pull away from her embrace. "Ma'am, uh—"

She smiles, tears pooling. "I owe you my life."

2

Passersby slow their pace, their curiosity piqued. People mill around, quietly murmuring as they gossip about what they just witnessed. All eyes on the coffee shop patio focus on me and the woman I saved.

Rather, the woman I poisoned.

No thought went into my actions, it was pure instinct. And I'd do it again given a chance. But now what?

She stares at me, doe-eyed with an open-mouthed grin. She might have a chance to survive if she gets to a hospital right away.

"Um, ma'am. Listen to me. I have..."

What do I say? I don't have time for explanations, and she won't believe me. I need to do something. I scan the area—for what, I don't know. Napkins from Starbucks? That won't work, but maybe water will.

"Stay right here," I tell the woman. "I'll be right back."

Her smile melts, and her eyes narrow. "Um...okay."

I sprint toward the coffee shop. My legs feel strong, my head no longer pulsates.

The transient man steps toward me. "Where you goin', hero?"

I look at him. Words escape me, but a glint of light behind him steals my attention. My shoes squeal on the concrete as I stop. I pivot and dart past him, then reach underneath the bench and grab his bottle of vodka.

"Hey, that's mine." He scowls but doesn't move.

I unscrew the top and jog back to the woman.

"What are you doing?" She steps backward and tenses.

"I have to sanitize you."

Her face contorts. "What?"

Before she can react, I pour the liquor over her bare shoulders and upper arms—any exposed skin I touched. I don't know how fast the virus absorbs into the skin, but with any luck, the vodka will kill it before it infects her.

She jumps back, her face twisted. "What the hell are you doing?" She wipes away the alcohol.

"No," I say. "You need—"

The crowd closes in around us, and an uneasy energy fills the air. "Hey," someone shouts. Another yells, "Leave her alone." Two men step out from the group, arms folded and scowling. "You okay?" one of them asks the woman.

I put my hands up and plead with her. "Please, you have to listen to me."

The woman takes another step back. "What is your deal?" Her fists are at her sides, knuckles white.

I survey the agitated mob. Several people hold their cell phones up, recording what might become the next viral social media post. I could walk away, continue living in my isolated existence, safe from anyone uncovering my past. I can't announce to the world that I have Grim Fever. But she deserves to know what I did to her.

With my hands up in a non-aggressive posture, I take a slow

step toward her.

She tenses.

I suck in a lungful of air. "I have to tell you something, but I can't say it in front of everyone."

She glares at me.

"You might have the Grim," I whisper.

She blinks but doesn't react.

One of the do-gooders from the crowd steps closer to me, eyes like a prowling tiger's. His red flannel shirt clings to his burly frame. With his bushy beard, he could be a model in a job ad for a lumberjack. "Hey bud, leave her alone."

"I'm not trying to hurt her. I'm trying to help." The words come out more aggressively than I intend. "Honestly," I say in a softer tone.

The woman's mouth opens, so only the tips of her teeth are showing. She looks me over, searching for something. "What are you doing? What do you want?" she asks.

I ease close enough for her to hear me without being invasive. "You might have Grim Fever," I say softly, hoping she heard me this time.

Her eyes bulge. She wraps her arms around herself and stumbles backward.

A flurry of nerves rumble in my gut. She heard it that time. I swallow the jagged mass in my throat. "You have to get to a hospital."

Her face goes vacant, lost in her thoughts with a million-mile stare. The crowd is silent, the whir of cars on the street the only sound. After a series of blinks, she comes back to reality. "I have the Grim?" The emphasis on 'Grim' carries through the assembly of on-lookers.

Audible gasps stream from the crowd. People scatter to put as much distance as possible between themselves and the woman in the tank top. Red-flannel-shirt-guy pushes a teenage girl to the ground as he flees. A few screams erupt as the crowd disperses.

Seconds later, no one is near us except for the homeless man. He shuffles toward me. Scowls. "Can I have my drink back, man?"

I hand the bottle to him. It's safe. I still carry the virus, but I'm not contagious at the moment.

The man draws a long pull from the bottle and wipes his mouth with his sleeve. "Thank you." He tilts the bottle toward me. "And you're welcome." He struts back to the bench.

I turn to the woman.

Her cheeks shine with tears, but she looks angrier than anything.

At the prison, I usually strike an intimidating or defensive stance. I fumble to appear non-threatening to this woman. Hands in pockets? To my side? I clasp my left hand over my right. "What's your name?"

"Lynn." She says it through clenched teeth.

"Nice to meet you, Lynn. I'm Chad. I know this is strange, but you need to be admitted to a hospital immediately." I slide my phone out to dial nine-one-one but freeze. I can't call. There will be questions that I don't want to answer. "Do you have a car nearby?"

She looks toward the street on her left, then shakes her head.

"Can I take you to the hospital?"

"No." She crosses her arms over her chest and steps back. "I'll call my husband." Her voice is steady once again, almost forceful now. She rubs the moisture from her cheeks. "Or my sister. She lives close."

I don't know if it matters at this point, but getting to the hospital sooner than later can only be a good thing.

She chews on the inside of her cheek.

My chin drops to my chest. I force out a sigh, a constriction in my chest challenging every breath.

Lynn juts her chin forward. "Do you...why would you say I have it? Grim Fever?"

"Because..." The words are thorns in my mouth. "Because I infected you."

She swallows hard, lines sear her forehead. "You infected me?" Her tone raises an octave.

"I'm sorry. But listen, the longer we wait, the more likely you're going to..." I can't say it aloud.

"Die?" Her voice cracks.

I grimace and nod. "I can explain everything to you, but you have to trust me."

Her eyes shrink into narrow slits. "Why would I trust you?" She sweeps her gaze from side to side. No one is around. Even the vodka-swilling man is gone. "I'm not going anywhere with you."

"I don't blame you." This is going nowhere, and time is crucial. Of course, she doesn't want to get into a car with a strange man. Especially one who just doused her in vodka. I blow out a sigh. "How long until your husband or sister can get here?"

She looks to her left again. "Maybe ten minutes."

"Okay, call one of them and get yourself to the hospital as soon as possible."

Lynn blinks, her face void of emotion. "I'll call my sister." She looks at her phone, but hedges. Her eyes meet mine. "How are you..." Her lips twist as she bites the inside of her cheek again.

"Alive?" I offer a sad smile.

"Yeah."

I shrug. "Wish I knew. But, once every month or so, I get these horrible headaches and rashes. My hands get incredibly sweaty; that's when it's most contagious. When I touched your skin, you were infected instantly. And my symptoms disappeared."

Lynn glares at me, scrutinizes me for any amount of bullshit, and she shakes her head. "I can't believe this."

"I know." I try to keep my voice steady. "It's weird. But please, call your sister and get to the hospital as soon as you can." I don't know if it will matter in the end, but maybe she'll have a chance if she gets in early.

"The news said it has a hundred percent fatality rate."

"Well, I'm still alive, and I've had it for two years."

Lynn inhales and fights back tears. She lifts the phone. "Kristin?" She squeezes her eyes shut. Her shoulders slump forward, and she grinds her palm on her forehead. "I'm so sorry, I forgot. Give my best to Ron and his family." She lowers the phone to her side. "I'm the worst. Today is her mother-in-law's funeral." She rubs the side of her head with her free hand.

"What about your husband?"

She snorts and looks away. "I don't have a husband. I just said that to...I don't know, scare you off or something."

Huh. "Is there anyone else you can call?"

She shakes her head. Her face loses color, and then the dam breaks, and her body shudders with every weep.

My heart sinks like a plummeting elevator. I don't know how to fix this. I open the Uber app on my phone. The nearest car is seventeen minutes away. "Okay. Call nine-one-one. Tell them you've been exposed to—"

"You really have it?" Her strained voice sounds painful.

I nod.

"And you're alive?"

"I am alive."

Her gaze feels like she's burrowing through my skull to read my thoughts. To determine my sincerity.

"Do you want me to call?"

She shakes her head. "I had a panic attack the last time I was in an ambulance."

"Well, maybe—"

She puts her hand up. "Where's your car?"

Lynn sits squished against the passenger-side door, her balled fist close to the handle. She looks straight ahead through the windshield but positions her head to keep me in her peripheral view.

I contemplate a plan for when we arrive at the hospital. Do I go inside with her? Offer support if she wants it? Or drop her off at the emergency entrance and drive away? That seems cold, but it suits my interests in maintaining anonymity.

The silence is discomforting. I clear my throat. "You doing okay, Lynn?"

She huffs a little laugh. "My name isn't Lynn. It's Lindsay. Lindsay Green."

Huh. "Well, Lindsay Green, my name really is Chad. Chad Chaucer."

I wait for a response—people always have something to say about my name—but she remains quiet.

"What made you decide to trust me?" I look ahead at the road but sense her turn toward me.

"I don't fully trust you." She inhales. "But the vodka...that was so weird. Like, you were genuinely panicking."

I let out a short chuckle. "I was panicking. Still am."

I sneak a peek at her; she's smiling.

"Is your last name really Chaucer?"

There it is.

"Yes. No relation to the writer. I know how weird it sounds, and I've heard all the jokes. My nickname all through high school was Cha Cha."

Lynn—Lindsay snorts. "That's amazing." She laughs to herself. "So, how...how did you find out you had it? The Grim."

"A little over two years ago, I went to the hospital with a one-o-four fever and debilitating body aches. I couldn't stand to pee, let alone walk. The doctor comes in—young guy, Doctor Morston. He tells me I have some sort of viral infection that's causing brain inflammation. He didn't seem concerned, thought it would pass. Two days later, I know I'm going to die. I felt my body withering. A plum-colored rash covered my entire body. I looked like Grimace from the old McDonald's commercials. I'm lying in the hospital bed, head throbbing, skin itchy as hell, sheets soaked from sweat, hands leaking like a hose."

I realize then I've never spoken these words to anyone. I relive the memory in my mind a dozen times a day, but saying the words aloud feels like a bear trap clamping on my heart.

Lindsay shifts in her seat. "You okay?"

"Yeah. Sorry." I fill my lungs with a deep breath. "So, I feel like I'm about to die. My wife, Leanne, comes to see me. I try to tell her I love her, but my mouth doesn't work. She takes my hand, and in that instant, all the horror evaporated—the rash, headache, sour joints, everything."

Lindsay sinks back into the headrest. "Wow."

"I was never spiritual, but I thought it was a miracle—that Leanne cured me with love." I pause to gather myself, so I don't end up irrigating my face with tears. "Turns out, I infected her. I felt, like, perfectly fine. No fever, no aches. But the next morning, Leanne was in the ER with all the same symptoms I had."

Lindsay leans toward me again. "Oh my gosh."

I grip the steering wheel, hands void of color. Moisture

collects in my lower lids. "She died five days later."

I blink and let the tears dribble down my face. Getting the thoughts out of my mind didn't ease the burning in my chest. Maya Angelou said every storm runs out of rain. After two years, I'm still waiting for this downpour to stop.

Another quiet spell haunts the cab of the truck. Lindsay's been quiet since I dropped my sob story on her. I wouldn't know what to say, either, if the roles were flipped.

Lindsay ahems. "What does it feel like?"

"Imagine you're under the scorching Death Valley sun on a July afternoon, dozens of scorpions are creeping over your bare skin, your brain is in a paint mixer, and someone has drilled holes in all your joints. That's the second day, and it only gets worse from there."

"Oh." Lindsay brings her feet up onto the seat and hugs her knees.

Damn. I shouldn't have dumped it on her like that. I gnaw the inside of my cheek. "I'm sorry. It'll probably be different for you. We're going to get you in early. It's only been, what, thirty minutes? Most people don't know they have it until the fever hits."

I almost believe it myself.

I pull onto the exit ramp, slowing as we approach an eighteen-wheeler at the stop sign. "I am truly sorry. I wish I could take it back. You don't deserve anything like this."

The hazard lights on the semi in front of us start blinking. The rig shutters and stalls, blocking the single lane. We are pinned, both shoulders of the road too narrow to pass. "Ah, damn it. Hopefully, this won't take too long."

"Chad?"

I turn to her. "Yeah?"

She makes circles on her palm with her index finger. "How many people have you...infected?"

An icy prickle permeates inside my chest. I'm not prepared to answer. "Um...I don't know."

Her lower lip trembles.

"Wait, let me explain."

Lindsay's face loses its color.

"Um, first was Leanne. Doctor Morston died right after her. That's two. And, uh, the rest were—"

"How many?"

"Twenty-three, twenty-four, maybe." I cringe when the words pass my lips.

"Twenty-four people? Did you drive each of them to the hospital, too?"

"No. I've been working as a corrections officer. I've, uh, infected murderers, rapists, horrible people like that." It's easy to justify in my mind, but speaking the thoughts out loud makes them seem far worse.

"You intentionally spread the virus to those people?"

"Yes, but only to the most despicable humans."

"That's murder." Her words are tangled in barbed wire. "You might have infected me by accident, but all those other ones? It doesn't matter if they're bad people, it's still murder." She's almost yelling. "Do you think you're a real-life Dexter or something? Some viral vigilante?" Her hand inches toward the door handle.

I shake my head. "No, I never wanted this. It's the only way." I turn, grab her eyes with mine. "I've tried to stop it. I've attempted suicide. More than once. But it's like I'm possessed. This goddamn virus...it takes hold and controls me."

Lindsay rubs the door handle with a finger, her eyes darting from me to the door like a wild animal debating fight or flight.

I fail to think of an explanation that doesn't make me sound like a psychopath. She's not my prisoner.

"You can get out if you want. The hospital is four blocks to the right."

Lindsay scratches her shoulder, eyes still boring holes in my skull. The familiar purple blotches have already formed; it's progressing faster than usual. She must notice the concern on my face. She looks at her arm, then back at me. Her ravenous glare is replaced by stark fear.

The rumbling of the semi pulls my attention. The rig trudges forward.

Lindsay sighs. "Can you just drive me, please?" She sounds like a reluctant teenager.

"Of course."

The rest of the ride is silent. We pull into the emergency entrance, and I gesture to the sliding glass door. "Do you want me to come in with you?"

"No." She's aged two decades during the short trip, her face grayed from the grim reality before her. She opens the door and slides out.

"Lindsay."

She peers up at me without lifting her head.

"If your hands get super sweaty, that's when the virus is most contagious. But the regular hospital gloves seem to be safe."

She sucks her upper lip and nods.

"Don't let them give you ibuprofen; it makes the pain and itching worse. And have them keep your room as cold as possible."

She rubs her arm and nods once. Her eyes focus on the ground.

I sigh. "I know it doesn't mean much, but I'm sorry. I am so sorry."

She shrugs and slams the door. With her shoulders slumped

forward and her chin at her chest, she walks into the hospital.

Leanne's face flashes in my mind. My last memory of her smile. I miss that smile.

Doctor Morston's concerned face is next. He had so many years of medicine ahead of him.

And now, Lindsay. I recall how she gave up her seat so the elderly couple could sit next to each other. Another young life I've cut short.

These are the ghosts that will forever haunt me.

A car blares its horn. I wave 'sorry' and leave the hospital parking lot, getting back onto the highway. With all the symptoms gone, I feel incredible, but guilt is eating me from inside out. I can't stop thinking about Lindsay, how I've effectively killed her by saving her from that speeding car. The silence in my truck makes me uneasy, so I turn on the radio.

"...this breaking report. Due to concerns regarding the SVE-1 virus, Governor Patterson has issued a state-wide health and safety order for the next two months, effective immediately. Full details can be found on the governor's web site, but we'll share a quick rundown of the two main points. First, all non-essential businesses are encouraged to close. Grocery stores are to remain open, but Starbucks has already committed to closing all of its locations. Second, the state urges all citizens to remain at home. If you need to go out into public, you are asked to wear rubber gloves and long sleeves. The governor's office stresses that these are not requirements, it's a voluntary quarantine, but if everyone does as they're asked, this disease will run its course, and we can get back to normal. Folks, watch out for that Grim Fever. It's going to be a long couple of months."

3

Grocery stores are barren three days into the governor's health and safety order. Dry pasta, meat, and milk are gone. Canned goods are cleared out save for one dented can of pinto beans; no, thank you. A sign taped to an empty shelf informs customers that paper towels and toilet paper won't be in stock for two more weeks. I picked up a few newspapers, just in case. I shudder at the thought.

My shopping list isn't the only thing the quarantine is spoiling. How am I going to find someone to infect when the time comes? The prison furloughed me, so that's off the table. Most businesses are closed except for grocery stores and gas stations, and the handful of people out and about mostly wear long sleeves, gloves, and masks. It's almost impossible to judge a person's character if they aren't interacting with anyone.

I've been wondering about people I know that have questionable morals. The only person I can think of would be Nick, another correctional officer at the prison. He sells drugs to the inmates, and he's a prick in general. I'm pretty sure he cheats on his wife, too. But she's pregnant, so I can't do that to her and the unborn child. I have a month to come up with a plan, so time is one thing I have working for me.

Maybe I'd consider Nick in an absolute emergency.

According to the last news report, the national death toll has surpassed ten thousand. Ten thousand deaths, all because of me. The weight of that knowledge overwhelms me. For the past two years, I tried to be careful in my selection of...victims? I hate using that term, but what else could I call them? The prison idea worked well at all of my previous stops, but somehow the virus escaped the walls of the Spokane Correctional Facility. I controlled this disease for two years, but I should have known it was inevitable for something this contagious and deadly to escape my grasp.

I wish I'd had the foresight to realize that every person I touched would infect others, and they'd infect even more. Whenever I think of the number of people I've killed with this virus, I envision Leanne's big brown eyes gazing at me from the end of a long tunnel. One by one, additional sets of eyes blink open like light bulbs switching on. The hall grows brighter, tens of thousands of eyes glaring at me until it's so bright I'm blinded.

Every time I close my eyes, Lindsay's face is there. I'm tempted to call the hospital, act like a relative checking on her, although I know what the response will be. After three days, she's in agony with the worst imaginable itch and excruciating pain throughout her body. Her fever is probably a hundred and five, at least, and her sheets are soaked-through only minutes after changing them. The rash envelops her skin, giving her the appearance of a bleeding eggplant. At this point, she'll imagine her only relief will come with a swift death. Worse than knowing I essentially killed her is the unforgettable image of her face before she walked into the ER. Her deep brown eyes, wide with fear and gloom, are seared permanently into my mind.

The rash on her arm came on so fast. What was that about? Symptoms usually take about twelve hours to manifest. At that rate, I wonder if she's still alive. I pull out my phone and find the number for the hospital. It rings twice.

"Spokane General Hospital," a woman says. "Please hold."

"Okay."

An acoustic guitar ballad serenades me as I wait. A moment later, the woman comes back on the line. "Thank you for holding. This is Monica, how may I direct your call?"

"Uh, hi. I'm calling to check on the status of a patient—Lindsay Green."

"I can't give you patient information over the phone, sir."

"Oh. I...okay."

Damn.

"Can I help you with anything else, sir?"

"No, thanks."

"Have a nice day."

"You, too."

I pull into the hospital's visitor lot and park. I'm happy to be out of the truck; the ride was terrible with watery eyes and a dribbling nose from the floral arrangement I picked up at the grocery store. Apparently, I'm allergic to chrysanthemums. Once inside, I approach the front desk.

A large woman with freckles and red-framed glasses sits behind the counter. She wears light blue exam gloves and a lavender mask tucked under her frames. She rolls her chair back. "How can I help you?"

I read her name tag. "Hi, Monica. I was wondering if you could give me the room number for Lindsay Green? She came in three days ago."

Monica pushes her glasses up her nose, her dubious green eyes fixed on me. She types without looking at the screen and clucks her tongue. "Did you call earlier?"

Should I act like I'm a family member? What was Lindsay's brother-in-law's name? Rob? Rich? I panic. "I...yes."

Smooth, Chad.

Monica's eyes shift. I'd wager that she's frowning behind the mask. "Lindsay Green is in the SVE-1 virus quarantine. No visitors allowed."

My shoulders go slack. "Oh. It won't be much longer, then."

Monica scoots forward and looks around. "I'm not supposed to say anything, but..." Her eyelids close in a drawn-out blink. "There are three Grim patients back there. None of them are expected to make it past tomorrow."

I wonder if Lindsay infected the other two patients. "Thank you."

"Be safe," she says.

I turn to leave, then pause. I turn around and offer the flowers to Monica.

Her eyes squint, her mask hiding a smile. "That's sweet, but we can't accept anything from outside."

"Oh, of course."

I dump the flowers in a trash can near the exit. Before I reach the door, the aroma of roasted coffee pulls me to a vending machine. I choose the largest size available and wait as it brews, the scent stimulating my nerves. I didn't realize I was exhausted until now.

The machine spurts and percolates, and I welcome the brief distraction from destroying Lindsay's life. When the brew finishes, I grab the cup and take a sip. The coffee isn't terrible—only slightly burnt—but it needs a few minutes to cool off.

The parking lot is mostly empty. I assume there aren't many visitors these days. I open the door and reach for the grab handle inside my truck, but the coffee cup slips from my other hand, bounces off the seat, and into my chest. The lid pops off, scalding java douses my shirt.

Damn it.

I pull my shirt off and climb into the seat. A red blotch in the shape of a pear glows on my chest.

A match strike of panic ignites beneath my ribs. Below the pear-shaped burn, a purple splotch blossoms.

4

Twenty-three states have confirmed cases of Grim Fever. Nineteen have closed their borders and enacted shelter-in-place directives, among those Idaho and Oregon, leaving me landlocked in the Evergreen State. Washington's governor hasn't modified the health and safety order, but that could change any day.

Interstate spread isn't the only surprise. The sweats and full-blown fever came back only six days after sharing the infection. Body aches and rash joined the party, too. I can't decide which is worse—the constant itch or my brain boiling inside my skull. I should have another three or four weeks before this happens, but for reasons unclear to me, it's early and as bad as ever. The virus must be mutating. Which means I need to figure out a plan fast.

The news reported resistance to the shelter-in-place orders, so there will be a handful of protests, which is my best chance of finding someone to infect. But how do I go about vetting them?

I set the air conditioner to sixty-two. Frigid air doesn't do much to ease the agony, but it's the only thing that is remotely effective. My head throbs. I think someone inserted a rat inside my brain, and it's burrowing its way out. Thinking makes the pain worse, so I shuffle into the living room and plop on the couch. Maybe something on TV will inspire me.

Happy Days reruns.

No.

Soap commercial.

Nope.

The Bold and the Beautiful.

Maybe later.

Blender infomercial.

No. Daytime television programming is less exciting than auditing an Intro to Philosophy course. I change the channel again.

Local news coverage of protestors outside the capitol building.

I leave it on. A male reporter stands about thirty feet from the crowd. He wears a surgical mask, safety goggles, blue medical gloves, and a rubber raincoat. "You can see two dozen protesters behind me. They claim that the health and safety order is unconstitutional and that the governor is a fascist."

That's funny. The governor's order explicitly suggested safety measures. There were no mandates, no enforcement for non-compliance.

Chants ring out from the crowd. "Hoax virus, false flag! Hoax virus, false flag!"

The reporter rolls his eyes, then nods once as he realizes he's still on camera. "As you can hear, these folks believe that the SVE-1 virus, which has killed thirteen thousand Americans, is a hoax."

I imagine him biting his lip underneath his mask, fighting the urge for personal commentary.

A potato-faced man with a scraggly beard approaches the reporter. He's wearing a white t-shirt emblazoned with a red, white, and blue eagle. "This is a false flag event," he says into the camera. "The government is flexing their muscles, showing how easy it is to send these sheep into their homes. Not me." He gestures to his fellow protestors. "Not us. We will not be intimidated. We will not allow those in power to use fear to control us."

"What is your name, sir?" The reporter angles his microphone toward the man.

"I'm Wade Linford, and I ain't no sheep."

He continues on a red-faced tirade, but I mute the TV and grab my laptop from the end table. A quick Google search on Wade Linford returns a trove of hits. He leads a group called Freedom Against Tyrannical Establishments—FATE. I read through dozens of anti-government social media posts that display his questionable literacy. A free online criminal search reveals a few drug-related arrests and an incident two years ago in which he was arrested for inciting violence at a counter-protest for a rival presidential candidate. And—

Holy shit.

Wade Linford was arrested six years ago for killing a Native American teenager in Oklahoma. I Google it and find several articles. In the police interview, Mr. Linford said he thought the boy was an illegal immigrant who stole something from a convenience store. Despite video evidence that showed Wade stalking after the boy with a pistol at his side, they dropped the charges for lack of evidence. The boy was unarmed unless you consider a Snickers bar a deadly weapon. The young man had the receipt in his pocket.

This is it. I have my target.

I pull up FATE's Facebook page. They are planning another protest tomorrow morning at the Post Office.

The tension in my neck relaxes, the thrumming in my head is now a quiet hum. Even the rash doesn't itch right now. It's like the virus knows I've found a target, and it's rewarding me with temporary relief.

This Walmart is as empty as a maple tree branch in January. Ten minutes in, and I've seen only one customer—a frantic man jogging toward the register with a box of diapers. The food section looks like the remains of a tornado-swept town. The hunting section is picked over, but some of the clothing racks are still standing. After a half-assed search, I pluck a long-sleeve camouflage shirt from its hanger and a pair of dark Wranglers. A red 'USA' trucker hat catches my attention, so I nab it from the end cap and smile. My ensemble is complete.

My phone rings, but I don't recognize the number, so I let it go to voicemail. I go through the self-checkout. The shirt and hat total seventeen bucks and some change. I need to keep track of these things now that I won't receive a paycheck for who-knows-how-long.

I get into my truck and plug my phone in. The screen lights up, and I remember the voicemail, so I tap the button and listen.

"Chad?" a woman's voice says. "I need you to call me back at this number as soon as you can. This is Lindsay Green."

5

My tires scream as they grip the asphalt, the stench of burnt rubber assaulting my nostrils. Four cars on the entire road, and I'm behind the one idiot who slams the brakes of his minivan for no apparent reason. "Asshole," I say through the windshield.

That'll show him.

Lindsay didn't answer when I called back, but I left a voice message. A surreal chill surrounds me. She can't be alive. In some crazy cosmic accident, another Lindsay Green contacted me. Right?

The jerk in the minivan turns off, so the street in front of me is clear. Typically, the evening rush hour would have me crawling on this road, but I'm cruising at a steady fifty-four and only ten minutes from my house. I'm not sure why I'm in such a rush to get home, but panic feels right at the moment.

Finally, the phone rings. "Hello?"

"Chad? I'm, like, shaking right now," Lindsay says—the Lindsay from a few days ago that should be dead right now. Her voice is crisp and lively, a vast difference from the last time

I heard her speak.

Relief flutters through me like a swarm of butterflies on meth.

"Tell me what happened." I feel like I'm talking to a ghost. "How are you—"

"I'm scared, Chad. There were these people that came to see me. I just...it didn't feel right." She's talking too fast for me to comprehend.

"Wait. What people?"

"A creepy red-headed guy with a goatee and an Asian lady in glasses. They're from the CDC."

"CDC? That makes sense. You survived a fatal disease, so it's not surprising that they'd want to talk to you."

"Yeah, but it seemed weird. Like, they really didn't care that I survived. They were more interested in...I don't know. They asked a bunch of questions, like if I've traveled out of the country, where I live, how I think I got infected."

My heart rate ratchets up. "What did you tell them?"

"I told them I didn't know. Don't worry—I didn't say anything about you."

Phew. "Did you get their names?"

"The guy's name was Mc-something, and the lady didn't say hers. But the weirdest part was that they wanted me to go with them to Atlanta. Like, immediately."

"That's where the CDC headquarters are."

"The red-headed guy said that. But the way he looked at me was scary. I don't know what it was, but I didn't trust him."

"You didn't trust me at first, but here we are talking."

"I almost died because of you."

Dang, that stings. "You're right," I say, shaken. "Uh, so what did you do?"

"I told them I needed to think about it, and they got pissed. The guy was screaming at me that millions of people would die because I wouldn't go with them. And the lady...she was freaky. She just sat there and glared at me like I called her kid ugly or something. Now that I think about it, I'm not sure she said anything the entire time."

"So, I assume you're not on your way to Atlanta right now with a freaky Asian woman and a red-haired guy?"

Lindsay huffed a little laugh. "No. I'm at my sister's."

"How did you get out of the hospital?"

"After they asked me all those questions, I said I needed to use the bathroom. I went, but I had a weird tingle in my gut telling me not to go back. I walked out the front door, found a guy smoking outside, and asked to use his phone. I called my sister, and she picked me up."

"What are you going to do now?"

"I don't know. That's why...I was hoping you would know what to do."

Huh. I'm flattered that Lindsay would think I'd have the narrowest idea of what to do, but I'm at a loss for words, let alone actions. I stumble over empty thoughts. The only thing I can think to say is, "How did you get my number?"

"Seriously? You think there are thousands of Chad Chaucers wandering around Spokane?"

I chuckle. "Fair point."

Any sort of solution eludes me. I'm not sure why she's so freaked out about the CDC; I wish I'd realized sooner that I should share my survival with medical professionals, but I'd infected dozens of people before I thought of it and worried I might be arrested. Maybe I can convince her to talk to them, so she doesn't tumble to the same level of guilt I've been living with. "Can you meet up to talk in person? I'm sure we can come up with something together."

Silence.

"Lindsay?"

A rustling noise. "Um, yeah. Okay." More rustling. "My sister is coming, too."

"Sounds good. How about the Starbucks where we met? It's closed, but we can meet up in the parking lot."

Lindsay huffs. "You have a thing for irony, don't you?"

She's funny. "I'll be there in fifteen minutes."

Lindsay talks to someone else away from the phone. A swishing sound comes from her end of the line, then, "'K, see you then."

The last two minutes of my life sent me chasing my thoughts in a tornado. I try to mentally catch up. Loneliness has been my only friend for the past two years, give or take a month, but Lindsay surviving gives me a glint of hope that I might have someone else around who understands. Unless she has to go to the CDC in Atlanta; then, I'll be stuck in solitude again. This is a dilly of a pickle.

The Starbucks is dark and empty. No patrons sipping macchiatos on the patio, no cars in the lot, just vacant asphalt. The only other person around lies asleep on the bench, his bottle wrapped tightly in his arms. I shift into park, and the service indicator illuminates on the dashboard. Overdue for a tune-up. Hell, my body could use a tune-up now that the headache has shifted into a steady vibration. The itchiness is making its way back, too, but still nowhere near as bad as earlier. I slide off the seat, shut the door, and lean against the fender.

Two minutes pass, then my phone buzzes. A new text message from Lindsay:

    Kristin doesn't know you infected me.

That's good to know.

Seconds later, a burgundy SUV pulls into the lot and parks two spots away from my truck.

I wave.

Lindsay gets out of the passenger door. She's wearing knee-length yoga pants and a mint green tank top, her hair pulled into a ponytail. Another woman, presumably Lindsay's sister, opens her door and peers over the roof.

"Chad, this is Kristin. Kristin, Chad."

Kristin waves curtly and gently presses her door closed. She immediately directs her attention to her phone, leaning on her elbows atop the SUV's hood. Her appearance differs from Lindsay's in just about every way—light caramel-colored hair at her shoulders, fair skin with freckles, and about six inches taller. The only common trait between the two is their deep brown eyes.

Lindsay approaches me. She looks so much more vibrant than when I saw her last. Granted, today she's not marching off to her deathbed. I'm not sure if I should hug her. I look at Kristin. She's eyeballing me like a pit boss behind a blackjack dealer.

"Hey," Lindsay says.

"Hi. Uh..." She's at arm's length. Here goes nothing. I extend my arms and lean in.

"Oh," she says, her voice peppered with surprise. She hugs me, giving two quick pats on my back, then releases. I look past her toward Kristin, who rolls her eyes and returns to her phone.

"I was thinking. Maybe it's best to talk to the CDC people. See if there's a way where you don't have to go to Atlanta."

Lindsay's mouth curls into a frown, and her eyes shift to the ground. "Oh."

"They probably want some blood samples to see how you

beat the Grim."

She shrugs, eyes still averted. "Kristin said the same thing."

Clearly, going to the CDC isn't her top choice. "They scared you that much, huh?"

Lindsay pinches her lips together and nods. "I don't want to see those people again. Maybe I can call my regular doctor."

"That's a brilliant idea," I say. "Tell me about the hospital visit. I'm sure they were going nuts when you pulled through."

She lifts her shoulder. "I guess. I think they were all more surprised than anything. One nurse even said I probably had a false positive test."

"What treatments did they give you?"

"They had me on antiviral medication—aycycle...Acyclovir."

That's what they gave Leanne right before her symptoms erupted.

Lindsay nibbles a fingernail. "The nurses and doctors said it was working better than any of the other patients, but then I guess it got worse. Like, way worse. You were right, it's the most horrific thing I've ever been through. I wanted to die."

"But you're alive."

"I'm alive."

She looks over her shoulder at Kristin, then back to me. Says in a low tone, "Can I ask you about...like, when you have to...you know."

I swallow hard. I knew this would come up. How much do I tell her? Do I go into detail about how I online stalked my next vict—person? I decide to let her ask questions and gauge my answers appropriately. "Ask me anything."

"You said it was every month that you have to..." She lets the words evaporate.

"Yes. Usually." I look at my glistening palms.

Her eyebrows squeeze together. "What?"

"I already have the symptoms."

She squints, then her eyes widen, and her jaw loosens as the realization hits home. "Oh my gosh. Right now? But—"

I nod. "I have a plan."

"A plan to kill someone?" she says in a harsh whisper.

"He deserves it. Trust me."

"Kristin's husband is a cop. Ron would arrest me if he knew—"

"I wish I could find another way, Lindsay."

Kristin pops her head up from her phone. "Linds," she says. "Let's go. Ron has to go to his dad's, and I need to get back to watch Maddie and David."

Lindsay looks at me, gnaws on her lower lip.

I swallow. "Do you, uh...I can drop you off." It comes out more like a question. "If you want."

"Hang on." Lindsay walks around to the SUV. Kristin stands upright, crosses her arms over her midsection. She looks less-than-pleased with what Lindsay has to say. Seconds later, Kristin gets in the SUV alone and starts the engine.

Lindsay comes back toward me as her sister leaves the parking lot. She smirks. "Kristin doesn't trust you."

"Do you trust me?"

Lindsay cocks her head to the side, squints one eye. "We'll see."

Heat blossoms on my cheeks.

"So, you have a plan?" she says.

I tell her about Wade Linford and FATE. How I'll go to the rally tomorrow and shake his hand. Lindsay's eyes narrow as she looks me over. I can't tell what she's thinking. "Google him," I say.

She pulls out her phone and finds an article covering Wade's murder of the Native American teen. Her mouth hangs wide open as she reads. Fury ignites in her eyes. "I hate to say it, but you're right—he deserves it."

We stand in silence. I don't want to be pushy, so I wait for her to gather her thoughts.

"I want to go with you," she says. "Tomorrow."

"To the protest?"

She nods.

"Okay. I don't think it'll be that exciting, though."

"I don't care. I want to see how you do it."

"All right. You got it." Her fitness guru outfits aren't going to cut it, though. "Do you have any clothes that would help you fit in at an anti-government protest?"

She looks to her left, down the street. "Maybe. My apartment is three blocks away. Let's go check."

The last time I was in this part of town, I was surrounded by two dozen people after dumping vodka on Lindsay. Now, the streets are empty. It's good to see most people taking the shelter-in-place order seriously. If I weren't the root cause for the spread of the disease, I'd lock myself away in my house, too. We reach the intersection where I pulled Lindsay away from the speeding car. She stops abruptly and puts her arm across my chest. "Watch out," she says. "This intersection isn't safe." She looks left then right in exaggerated movements.

I laugh so hard I have to put my hands on my knees, and Lindsay's ears turn tomato red as she belly chuckles.

I finally catch my breath. "You're right. Can't be too safe."

We cross the street—against the orange hand signal because there are exactly zero cars out right now—and head down the block. Two birds chatter on top of an awning.

"What did you do before you got the virus?" Lindsay asks. "For work, I mean."

"I coached high school soccer and taught driver's ed." I miss the simplicity of my old life. "What about you?"

"I'm a network engineer, and I volunteer at the Spokane Reservation a few days a month teaching technology to the elementary kids."

"Wow. That's fantastic."

"Yeah."

"What drove you to volunteer?"

"No one gives those kids a chance." Her voice is stern. "They're mostly left to fend for themselves. The parents try, but there's a major substance abuse problem. I never lived on the reservation, but I have cousins there. I try to do my part to help."

"I didn't realize—"

"I'm half. My dad is white." She's annoyed like she's had to explain this a thousand times.

I grimace. "Forgive my ignorance."

She shakes her head and twists her lips. "No, it's okay. So, what do you do for fun?"

I huff. "Not much anymore. I read a lot, watch Netflix. Pretty boring existence. I used to play in a co-ed soccer league with my wife. And we took weekend trips with two other couples that we played with." I kick a loose pile of mulch from the sidewalk back into its place. "But I try not to get close to people now."

Lindsay sighs.

Her life will change, and I bet it's hitting her now. The kids she works with, her sister's family...everything will have to change.

"What did you tell your sister about me?"

Lindsay smirks. "I told her we just started seeing each other." Her face stiffens, and she quickly adds, "Don't get any ideas; it was just a cover story."

I nod, unsure of what to say.

We walk in silence for another block, then turn a corner. Lindsay points to a modernized four-story brick building with long, narrow windows. "Here we are."

"Nice. You like it here?"

"Eh. Looks better on the outside." She points to a balcony three floors up. "That's my place."

Flowerbeds bookend the path leading to an exterior stairwell. Bright pink puffy things, white...tulips, maybe, and...chrysanthemums. Yuck. I follow Lindsay up the steps. I'm looking down at my feet—as a gentleman does when following a lady up stairs—and we collide awkwardly. I didn't see her stop.

"Shoot," she says in a panicked whisper. "Go back down. Now."

I turn and take three steps at a time. "What's wrong?"

"Just go."

I reach the bottom of the stairs.

Lindsay blows past me, trampling through the flowers and around a corner.

I follow. When I come around the corner, she's ten yards ahead of me in a dead sprint and racing toward the parking lot. I haven't put the old legs into this gear in a while, and my knees creak with every step.

Lindsay ducks behind a half-wall. I finally catch up, winded like I just finished a ninety-minute soccer match. I round the corner and let gravity tug me to the grass. "What the hell's going on?" I struggle to get the words out through my out-of-shape breathing.

Lindsay's eyes are wide, her breaths deep but controlled. She shakes her head.

"Are you okay?"

"I saw him—that CDC guy. He was at my door."

It makes sense the CDC would want to track her down. She

could help them find a cure for this awful disease—which, selfishly, would make my life easier. But something about the guy has her terrified.

"You're sure it was him? Not a neighbor, or—"

"Yes. I'm sure." She looks at me, visibly annoyed. "There are only four apartments up those stairs. Mine, two vacant ones, and a miserable old man that never has visitors." Her jaw stiffens. "It was him."

"What do you want to do? I can take you back to your sisters."

Lindsay looks beyond me, not focused on anything in particular. "I don't want to get Kristin involved. She's already annoyed with me, and having government people track her down would put her over the edge. She would never speak to me again."

"Do you have anyone you can stay with?"

She shakes her head, yanks a few blades of grass out of the ground.

A minute passes.

Words are lost on me.

Lindsay sighs. Her eyes dart up at me, and she shrugs. "Well..."

6

Lindsay lies dead asleep on the couch, curled in a fetal position. The throw blanket is tucked under her chin with her baby blue socks peeking out from the bottom. I'm glad she could get comfortable.

I open the cabinet and pull out a coffee mug, trying to be as stealthy as possible. I wonder if Lindsay drinks regular coffee, or if she strictly drinks the sweetened Starbucks beverages. I check on her to see if the coffee maker woke her, but she hasn't budged. I make myself a bowl of cereal and eat in silence while re-reading my favorite Gillian Flynn novel. The book helps me escape reality, where every cell of my body either itches or hurts.

I'm deep into the book when Lindsay pops her head up from the couch.

I glance at the clock—eight twenty-six. "Good morning," I say.

"Morning." Her voice is scratchy, hair a disorganized puzzle.

I hold up my empty mug. "Want some coffee?"

She shakes her head. "Can I have some water, please?"

"Of course." I pour a glass of water and take it to her. "How'd you sleep?"

"Good." She downs half the water without coming up for breath, then lets out a satisfied sigh. She pushes down on the seat cushion. "Your couch is comfy."

"You hungry? I have little to offer besides frozen waffles and Lucky Charms. Or I can make eggs."

"I'm okay for now. Thanks." She looks at the recliner where she put last night's Walmart purchase—a red USA t-shirt and Wranglers. "What time is the protest?"

"Noon. We have about three hours until we need to leave."

She gulps the rest of the water. "Mind if I take a shower?"

"Not at all. I put a towel on the counter in the hall bathroom."

Lindsay thanks me and gets up, arches her back and stretches, then grabs her protest clothes. She catches me watching her, smiles, and disappears into the hall.

I shower and dress in my room. The Wranglers are stiff, which amplifies the rash. I might as well wrap my body in Saran Wrap. I head out to the living room just as Lindsay comes out of the bathroom dressed in her red shirt and jeans. Her hair lays straight, a few inches past her shoulders. The way it frames her face changes her entire appearance. In a pleasant way.

"Look at us," I say. "Couple of regular old government-hatin' patriots."

Lindsay laughs. "Ugh. These jeans are so tight." She raises her leg to stretch the denim. "This is going to be annoying."

I rub my hands on my pants. "A bit starchy, aren't they?"

"Yeah. I should have got a size larger. Oh, well. I'll make it work. Can I have a bowl of Lucky Charms?"

"You got it."

I sit at the table with her and continue reading my book. Lindsay's spoon clanks against the bowl. I've never had someone inside my home. Hell, I haven't had anyone I'd call a friend since I left Philadelphia.

An image of Leanne enters my mind. The cabin we rented in the Poconos with the Fletchers. We'd sit around the fire, drinking wine and laughing. The last trip we took before—

"Should I put this in the sink?" Lindsay says.

"Sure. Thanks." The memory evaporates.

"What should we do while we wait?"

I'm not used to entertaining. "I...don't know. Watch a movie?"

"Sure. What do you like?"

I lift the book and show her the cover. "Dark thrillers, mostly. What about you?"

"I like anything. I could go for something dark."

We settle on *Gone Girl*.

We make light conversation on the drive to the protest, though the sobering reality of what I'm about to do lingers below the surface. We approach the post office, and we're directed to an area lined with orange and white barricades. We park two blocks away. Signs bob above the roofs of the vehicles in the lot. 'Lockdown Is A Scam,' 'Sheep Get Slaughtered,' and my favorite, 'Grim Fever Is A Hoxe.' Misspelling isn't a crime punishable by death, I remind myself.

We fall in line with a group of about twenty folks marching toward the post office. Some are chanting, others remain stoic. Lindsay leans close to my side, her shoulder pressed against my arm. I scan the crowd for Wade Linford, but he looks so similar to most of the men here that it's become something of a needle in a haystack search.

Police presence is heavy despite the small crowd. No one is subject to arrest for disobeying the health and safety directive since it's technically a suggestion. But with or without my presence, everyone here is at risk of infection. I thought perhaps the police were here to keep the peace if an opposing group showed up, but the only instance of a counter-protest is a sign stuck into the ground that reads, "I would counter-protest, but I'm being socially responsible and staying home."

I think I have a new favorite sign.

We're led like cattle through barricades into a corral that abuts the post office property. I expect shoving and jostling for position, but most people are respectful of personal space. Still, Lindsay leans into me. Three men make their way to the front of the crowd. Wade Linford stands in the middle, holding a bullhorn. The group is small enough, though, that he doesn't need it.

"Hello," Wade says, the bullhorn to his side. "Thank you all for coming out and supporting your God-given right to assemble." Hoots and whistles ring out. "But the government," he says the word as if it's poison on his tongue, "wants us all to believe that ordering us to stay in our homes is for our own protection." More cheers. "I say bullshit. They're trying to put martial law in place." Even louder cheers.

I look at Lindsay. She's gritting her teeth and clenching her fists.

"Easy," I say. "We need to fit in here."

She rolls her eyes and unclenches her jaw.

Wade continues, "We can't fault the sheeple staying home for falling for the lies of big government. We need to educate them that this so-called virus is a hoax and that the supposed deaths are made up." Shouts fill the air. "Don't blame our brothers and sisters for being unenlightened. Blame the govern—"

A crack followed by the scattering of glass shards interrupts Wade. He flinches and spins toward the sound. A window in the post office behind him has a stone-shaped hole in it.

"Fuck the government," a man yells. The crowd shifts, fists pump in the air, and the brief silence following the broken window is replaced by a medley of chants and commotion.

Lindsay grabs my hand.

I panic at her touch, but I've already infected her.

"I don't like this," she says, her voice streaked with alarm.

"Me neither." I squeeze her hand and try to pull away from the teeming hoard, but a hefty man behind us with a wispy beard shouts, "Down with the Feds!" and pushes his way forward, knocking Lindsay to one side and me to the other.

"Chad!"

Police whistles shriek in my ears and a flurry of swinging nightsticks rains down on the penned-in crowd.

"Hang on," I say, but my shout is drowned out in the mayhem.

A scrawny guy wearing a gas mask shoves Lindsay. She lands hard on her knees.

I want to grab him by the throat, crush his larynx, infect him with my curse. Instead, I ball my fists to avoid touching anyone and use my elbows to swim-move through the rushing crowd. But I'm working against the undertow, tugged and pushed and pulled further away.

I can't get to Lindsay.

I'm knocked side to side, back and forth like a buoy in a storm. I duck under an exposed hairy gut, and spot Lindsay on all fours, bracing against the swaying sea of chaos. I fight to get to her, but I'm stuck. When a break in the crows opens up, she pops up like a boxer off the mat and shoves the lanky jerk who pushed her, knocking him to his ass. She snarls like a starving wolf, throws an elbow to the temple of a bald guy with neck tattoos, and kicks another man in the kneecap, sending him to the ground in a heap.

Damn. Does she train with Ronda Rousey?

Lindsay surveys the assembled mass, finds me, and gestures toward the back of the corral. I nod and turn, side-stepping a college-aged boy holding a baseball bat. I lunge forward and hurdle the barricade. I don't see the cop to my left until he swings his nightstick. An explosion of pain rifles through my shoulder. I nearly crumble. "I'm trying to leave, man."

"Get the fuck out of here, prick."

I want to tell him I'm not one of them, but what's the point? I move to the other side of the coral where Lindsay should be. My collarbone throbs, hot with pulsating blood flow. I move it around in a small circle. Hurts like hell, but I don't think anything's broken.

Police are wrangling the rowdy protestors while a man in the back records it on his phone. "Fascists," he hollers. This is exactly what these people want.

I search for Lindsay, but there are too many red shirts in the crowd. I spot a police officer with a woman wrapped in his arms, dragging her backward. I dash toward him when I realize he has Lindsay.

"Hey," I yell. "Let her go."

The officer reaches for his gun, his other arm pinning Lindsay against his chest.

I hit the brakes and put my hands up in front of me. We stare at each other for countless beats. Neither of us knows what to do amidst the mayhem. I'm soaked in sweat, terrified I'll puke with no warning.

Someone shouts, "Hey," and a brick-sized rock flies from the direction of the voice and slams the officer in the cheek. His head flings to the side, and he drops onto the sidewalk.

Lindsay runs to me, wraps her arms around me. "Holy shit.

Let's go."

"Yeah."

This couldn't have gone worse. My hands are oozing sweat. I need to pass the infection on. I could grab any one of the protestors, but doing that without knowing what type of person they are...I just can't. We walk toward the lot, a smattering of police eyeing us. I try to play cool, but the pain writhing in my shoulder is intolerable. I try to hold back from letting the agony show on my face.

We reach the parking lot and search for my truck. We walk through a few rows before I see it. I open my mouth to speak when Lindsay grabs my arm.

"Chad. Look." She points to a red pickup with massive oversized tires. Four men stand by the tailgate.

Wade Linford is among them.

I look at Lindsay, and she nods her head toward the men. "Go."

I suck up my last bit of energy and walk toward them. "Mr. Linford?" I say when I'm ten feet from his truck.

Wade tosses a bundle the size of a baseball into the bed of the truck. He turns, mouth pursed, eyes like a rabid dog. Two of the other men reach behind their backs.

I slow my pace, put my hands up. "I just want to thank you for all you've done. For FATE helping to educate those sheeple." I have an urge to rinse my mouth out after saying the words.

"Yeah?" He exchanges glances with the other men and nods. They each fold their hands in front of themselves, and the third man walks away. "Well," Wade says, "thanks for supporting the movement. What's your name?"

I say the first name that pops in my head. "Gil. Gil Flynn."

Wade extends his hand. "Nice to meet you, Gil."

An electric pulse flows through my fingers. I grab his hand

and shake.

He pulls his hand away, his mouth turned like he's just sucked on a rotten fish.

"Sorry," I say. "A little sweaty after a tussle with a cop."

Wade grins. "It's all right, brother. I have to get back to some business here, but I appreciate your kind words."

I walk back to Lindsay, and vigorous energy floods my body. I feel like I'm striding on cloud tops.

The euphoria dwindles, but I feel as fresh as a newborn despite the throbbing in my shoulder.

Lindsay has been quiet for most of the ride. "You okay?" I say.

"Yeah." She draws circles on her palm with a finger. "Reliving the moment."

"That was intense. You're a fighter, though."

"No, I..." She sighs and lets the words evaporate. She clears her throat. "So, are you, like, better now?"

I nod. "I feel like a new person." Hopefully, it lasts longer than eight days this time.

We turn onto my street. A cup of coffee sounds amazing right now.

"So that Linford guy will die in a few days?" Lindsay says.

"Yes."

She exhales through her nose. "But what if he doesn't? What if he's like me?"

"He's not like you. You're special. Besides, we got you into the hospital right after you were inf—"

"Who's that?"

A black sedan is parked in front of my house.

"Oh, shoot." She unbuckles and dives down onto the floorboard.

"What are you—" Then I see what scared her.

A man wearing a black suit steps out of the sedan, sunlight gleaming in his copper hair.

7

"Stay down," I say. "I'll get rid of them."

Lindsay pinches her eyes shut, draws in long breaths through her nose, and exhales slowly through pursed lips.

I pull into my garage and shut off the truck. "Stay in here and don't peek out."

"Okay."

I slide out of the truck. The red-haired man walks up my driveway. "Good afternoon. I'm Alex McNulty." He reaches a hand forward.

I shake his hand. He's safe; the virus is dormant after I infected Wade Linford. "Can I help you with something?"

"Do you know a Lindsay Green?"

"Yes."

"Do you know where she is?"

"Nope."

McNulty frowns. "How do you know her?"

"We met the other day at Starbucks." Apparently, I'm playing Two Truths and a Lie.

"When was the last time you spoke with her?"

I cross my arms over my chest. Classic power move. "What's this about?"

"I'm with the CDC. I just want to talk with Ms. Green."

"CDC?"

"We think she may have contracted SVE-1."

Cue the acting skills. "Whoa. Grim Fever?"

"Yes. It's important we find her."

"She's going to die. Why are you worried about her?"

"We want to find her because we believe she survived."

"Really? And how did you find me, exactly?"

"We traced a call from her cell phone to yours."

"The CDC traces phone calls now?" I hope Lindsay isn't using her phone right now.

"We do when it can help end an epidemic."

"Sorry, Mr. McNair. I don't know where she is."

"It's McNulty. Have you had physical contact with Ms. Green?"

Yes, I say in my head. "No," I say out loud.

"You're sure? No handshakes, hugs, or anything of that nature?"

"I'm sure. We chatted at Starbucks, exchanged numbers. I haven't seen her in person since."

He eyes me as if he's appraising a painting for an auction house.

"Okay, Mr. Chaucer. She has my contact information. Please have her get in touch with me."

"I don't think I'm ever going to talk to her again."

McNulty glares at me doubtfully.

I shrug. "I'm not going near anyone who has the Grim."

McNulty huffs through his nose. "Well, if you happen to speak to her again..." He lets the words linger, turns, and walks toward his car. A tiny woman I hadn't noticed before sits in the passenger seat, her head barely visible behind the dashboard.

She holds up a hand, and McNulty stops. The woman gets out of the vehicle and approaches him. Must be the woman Lindsay described. She says something to McNulty.

He spins, and together they approach me. "Mr. Chaucer," McNulty says. "This is Dr. Choi. She would like you to call Lindsay and give me the phone, so I can speak with her."

"No." The word flies off my tongue like a dart.

McNulty looks at the doctor. She nods once. He steps into my personal space.

I don't flinch.

"We know you drove Lindsay Green to the hospital."

His breath smells like hot onions. I nearly flinch.

"We can play this your way," he says. His onion vapor assaults my nose. "But you won't like that outcome, Mr. Chaucer."

"Since when does the CDC make threats to civilians?"

"Since now."

That wasn't as intimidating as I'm sure he hoped it would be. "Since you have no authority to carry out your threats, I'm asking you to please get off my property."

McNulty looks at Choi.

She blinks and turns toward their car.

"You're making a gigantic mistake," McNulty says. "You're putting lives in danger."

I shrug.

McNulty huffs through his nostrils. "If you hear from Lindsay Green, please encourage her to contact me." He reaches into his coat pocket. The jacket lifts momentarily, and I spot a gun holstered on his waist. He hands me a card.

"I'll see what I can do, Mr. McNealy."

He glares at me, nostrils flaring. Dr. Choi taps his elbow, and they both retreat to their car.

When did the CDC start arming its employees?

After the black sedan turns the corner, I go back into the garage and open the driver-side door of my truck. Lindsay looks up at me, eyebrows furrowed.

"They're gone," I say.

She shuts her eyes and sucks in a deep breath.

"The guy—McNulty—had a gun."

"What? Why would the CDC need guns?"

"That's what I thought. We need to get rid of our phones."

"Why?" She opens the door and gets out. "Are they tracing my calls or something?"

"Yep. They found my number on your call log. That's how they found out where I live."

Lindsay groans. "This makes no sense. I knew there was something weird with them."

"I don't know what the hell is going on. All I can figure is, if they can trace calls, they can probably track the location of a phone. And yours is right here."

"But they didn't know I was here."

I shrug, then grab a hammer from my workbench and set my phone on the ground, screen up. I lift the hammer over my head and—

"Wait," Lindsay says. "Can't we just hide them somewhere? Then if they try to track us, it'll lead them to wherever the hiding spot is?"

That's a much better option than smashing a thousand-dollar device. "Great idea. Where can we hide them?"

"I don't know." She looks at the ceiling, eyes trailing from side to side in deep thought. Her finger draws circles on her palm again. "Do you have a post office box?"

I shake my head. "No. I have a locker at the prison, but that won't work."

Lindsay cocks her head. "We could hide them in my office downtown."

"Can you get in?"

She sucks in air through her teeth. "My badge is at home. Dang."

I wrack my brain for an accessible spot that would be safe for a phone for—crap, how long will this go on?

"Let me call my sister. I don't want to get her involved, but maybe Ron can help."

I swallow hard. "Are...are you going to tell him everything?"

"I won't tell him about you. But I will tell him about those CDC jerks."

We go inside, and Lindsay calls her sister. I get the impression that it's not going well. Lindsay is defensive and apologetic, tears threaten to irrigate her cheeks. I don't know what brother-in-law Ron can do for us, but I hope it's something because Lindsay is putting herself in a tough spot with her sister.

I sit on the couch and turn on the TV. News coverage of strict lockdowns across the nation is endless. They display a map with a red overlay of areas struck by Grim Fever. The country looks like a paintball target. I thought I was being careful, limiting those I infected to restricted areas. I don't know where I went wrong, but clearly, I wasn't as careful as I thought.

Or are there others like me out there?

Lindsay says, "Thank you," and ends the call. She lumbers into the living room and collapses onto the other end of the couch.

I mute the TV. "How'd it go?"

Lindsay exhales like she's blowing out candles. "Kristin is pissed. She said I should have just gone with the CDC people."

"I take it she didn't understand your concern with them."

"No. She said I'm being paranoid and unreasonable." She shakes her head. "Maybe I am. I don't know."

"Well, the guy was carrying a gun, so I think you're right to be worried. What about Ron?"

"Today is his first day back on duty since his mom died. Kristin doesn't want to call him now, but she said she'd talk to him when he gets home tonight."

"Well, at least that's something."

Lindsay looks at the TV. She moves her hand over her mouth. "Oh, shoot."

The crawler at the bottom of the screen reads, "BREAKING NEWS: State-wide lockdown to be strictly enforced effective immediately. Governor orders all citizens of Washington to remain indoors."

I turn up the volume.

"...from his home, Governor Patterson has issued a lockdown for the entire state of Washington. The mandate requires all citizens to shelter in place with few exceptions: first-responders, including EMT, police, and firefighters; hospital staff; and essential city, state, and county maintenance employees. Also, a limited number of shipping and delivery staff will be allowed to work."

"This is crazy," Lindsay says.

The reporter continues, "Essential employees will receive documentation to enable them access to travel to and from work. All others must remain indoors. Anyone walking or driving will be stopped and questioned. Police have strict orders to arrest violators. The order follows a violent protest by the hate group FATE. Representatives of Governor Patterson declined to comment whether the mandate is in reaction to the actions from earlier today. No word yet on when the mandatory lockdown will end."

"Well, so much for hiding our phones," Lindsay says.

"Shoot. Maybe we'll get lucky and McNulty and Choi will try to come here and get arrested on the way."

Lindsay huffs. "That would be nice."

The lockdown forces Lindsay to stay here with me. I don't mind, but she has no clothes or personal items. I hope I have enough food for both of us. "Hey, I'm sorry you're stuck here with me."

Lindsay twists her lips and lifts an eyebrow. "Could be worse. I just wish I had more clothes. And a toothbrush. And my blow dryer and hairbrush. And make-up." She slumps forward. "Ugh, this is going to suck."

"I have an extra toothbrush, and you're welcome to anything in my closet to wear. I hear baggy is in style these days." I offer a cheesy grin.

She smirks. "Thanks. Got any ladies' underwear?"

It feels good to laugh.

We sit in a lull. "Want a drink? I think I have Sprite, apple juice, and orange juice."

"Got anything a little more adult?"

More laughs. "Yeah. Beer, tequila, or vodka?"

"How about a screwdriver?"

"You got it." I get up and make the drinks. I'm not much of a bartender, but I can handle mixing orange juice and vodka. I go back into the living room and hand Lindsay her drink.

"Thanks." She reaches for the glass. Her fingers brush my hand.

They're warm and moist.

8

Lindsay's symptoms have exploded. Her temperature is one-o-four, and the rash has crept up her neck. She's miserable, unable to move on her own without screaming like she's being tortured. Cold bathwater gives her the only semblance of relief, and even then, she's in agony. She doesn't say much lately, but her eyes tell a story of misery.

When I'm not tending to Lindsay, I spend my time trying to construct a plan for her. I have no success. Utterly helpless. The virus is furious, presenting itself with an intensity I've never seen. I did this to her. And with the lockdown, it's unlikely I'll find someone for her to pass the curse on to. Guilt punches through me like needles into a pincushion.

I've worked through several scenarios to help her, but haven't thought of anything realistic. If we could leave without the threat of arrest, our options would — wait, maybe that's it.

I stride into the bathroom where Lindsay lies in the tub, fully clothed in the cool water. "What if you go out in public, get yourself arrested? Then you can find someone to touch when you're locked up."

Lindsay glares at me, eyes rimmed in red. She grits her teeth. "What if I touch a cop?"

She's right. Too much risk in touching someone innocent.

Watching her go through this is worse than experiencing it myself. If I could steal her fever, itching, and aches, I would. And as terrible as the situation already is, we have to worry about the CDC. They might have immunity from the lockdown order.

Ron called Lindsay yesterday. Apparently, the CDC has a surveillance division for disease breakouts like this. He wasn't aware of any provision for them carrying firearms, but he said agencies like that sometimes have leeway in extreme circumstances.

I wish I could find some freaking leeway.

Lindsay sloshes in the water. She presses her hands on either side of her neck.

"Itch getting worse?"

She groans. "It feels like fire ants are having a picnic on my skin."

I'm shocked at how fast her symptoms flared up. I fear the virus has mutated into a more aggressive version of itself. So even if we can find someone for her to infect, it might be a quick turnaround before she has to do it again. I wonder if our best chance is for both of us to go to the CDC, despite the questionable nature of their field agents. It might be the only way for either of us to feel normal again. Plus, Lindsay might be given a chance so she wouldn't have to intentionally infect anyone and carry the burden of guilt I live with.

I leave the bathroom and grab McNulty's card from the kitchen counter. I'd be doing Lindsay a favor, right? She doesn't deserve to live how I have for the past two years. She deserves to have her life back.

I enter McNulty's number, then clear it. I flick his business card. Why can't I bring myself to call him? Lindsay's suspicion isn't unwarranted—I felt a negative vibe from him, too.

Damn it. I miss childhood when Mom or Dad would always have a solution and make things better. I want someone to tell me what to do.

"Chad," Lindsay cries out.

I run into the bathroom. She looks at me with sheer dread painted on her face. "I want to die."

"I know, it's the worst."

"No. I want—" She blows out a slow breath. "I want you to kill me."

9

"I can't kill you, Lindsay." My voice cracks.

"It's worse than the first time." She rubs her temples. "So much worse. I can't do this."

"We'll figure something out."

Lindsay squeezes her eyelids together, her mouth curls into the shape of a rainbow. She shakes her head. "No, we won't. And I don't want to kill anyone. No one should suffer like this."

"Hang in there." I realize that's the most ridiculous thing to tell somebody.

"Don't tell me to hang in there." She groans. "Can I have that bottle of vodka?"

In my experience, alcohol made the rash more irritating, but I'm not about to argue with her. "You bet."

I fetch the bottle, remove the cap. "Oh, let me get you a —"

Lindsay nabs the bottle from my hand, chugs straight from it. She downs a quarter of it before coming up for breath.

"Never mind."

She gulps another mouthful and swallows hard. "You don't

have anything else, do you?"

"Tequila or beer?"

"I mean—" She winces. "Weed. Painkillers. Anything stronger."

I shrug. "Sorry."

If dispensaries aren't essential businesses in a time like this, they should be. I never thought of trying marijuana to ease the symptoms, but it might work. The problem right now is acquiring it. The lockdown forced all the stores to shutter. I'm sure there are still dealers out there who sell to kids under twenty-one, but all the drug dealers I know from the prison are in lockup.

Wait...all but one.

I swipe through my phone contacts and find Nick Ansley. He wasn't shy about selling drugs to the inmates. He mostly sells stuff he picks up from dispensaries, but after three heroin overdose deaths among the prisoners, the word was that Nick started selling harder stuff. I'll call him to see if he has any weed and if he'd be willing to meet up.

The phone rings three times, then:

"Hello?"

"Hey Nick, it's Chad. From the prison."

"Oh. What's up, man?"

"Uh, I was calling to see if you had any—"

A woman's voice in the background calls for Nick.

"Hang on," he says.

His wife is eight months pregnant. It might be a longshot to get him out of the house, but maybe I can pick it up at his place. What is his wife's name? Sarah? Stacy? Samantha, that's right.

"Sorry, man, lady's bugging me. So what's up?" He sounds tipsy.

"How's your wife doing? Baby's due in a few weeks, right?"

"Uh...yeah." Nick sighs. "Anyway, why're you calling me?"

"Do you have any edibles or something you'd be willing to sell?"

He laughs. "Yeah, man. I have a ton of stuff. I didn't think you were into it, though"

"It's for my...girlfriend." I cringe, hoping she didn't hear me.

"All right, all right. How much do you need?"

"Uh, five gummies?"

"Okay. Dosage?"

Shit. I don't know this stuff. "Let's start low."

"All right. I got some ten-milligram gummies."

"Sounds good." I hope.

"So how—" The woman in the background screams at Nick. "Fuck off, Jacky! I'm on the phone. Jesus Christ. Sorry, man. So how am I gonna get this stuff to you?"

Jacky is definitely not his wife. But that's not my concern.

"Uh, I'm not sure. Lockdown puts a damper on things. Are you able to get out of the house?"

"Hell yeah. Kinda need to get out, if you catch me." He rasp-laughs. "How soon you need it?"

"The sooner, the better."

"All right. Um, you know Graham's Hardware Supply? The one by the hospital?"

"No, but I can look it up."

"Okay. When can you get there?"

"If it's near the hospital, maybe thirty or forty minutes. How much will it cost?"

"Call it a hundred even—need to factor hazard pay. Cash or Venmo, whatever's easiest for you."

"Okay. You still driving that blue Jeep?"

"Yep. I'll see you there."

The call ends.

I'm certain a hundred bucks for five gummies is quite a bit more than I'd pay at a dispensary, but I'm in a bind, and

Lindsay deserves whatever peace I can provide her. Water sloshes—Lindsay is moving. When I get to the doorway, she's standing in the tub.

I grab the towel from the counter and hand it to her.

"Sick of the water?"

She nods, wiping water from her soaked yoga pants.

"I just got off the phone with a...well, not really a friend, but an acquaintance at the prison. He's going to sell me some edible gummies."

Lindsay stops drying herself and looks at me, expressionless.

Is this a good blank stare, or a bad one?

"Did—do you still want something more than vodka?"

Lindsay resumes patting herself with the towel. "I don't know." Her voice is low and strained. "I've only done marijuana like, three times. Drugs scare me after seeing what my cousins have gone through."

"Oh. So, should I call him back?"

She shrugs. "How are you going to get them, anyway? Do you trust this guy?"

Not really. "Yeah."

Judging by the side-eye she's casting at me, she doesn't believe the lie.

"I don't know," I say. "He's actually kind of a sleaze bag. He left his pregnant wife, sells drugs to inmates. Pretty sure he's ripping me off for the five gummies I asked him for."

Lindsay braces herself on the wall and gingerly lifts one leg after another over the edge of the tub. "And you're friends with this guy?"

"No. Honestly, the only reason I have his number is because I picked him up for a shift once."

"Well, he sounds like a terrible human."

He is terrible. "Wait. What if we can treat you with

something better than a little THC?"

Lindsay comes out of the bathroom wearing her clothes from the protest, hair still damp. "I don't think I can do it, Chad." She scuffs across the floor and drops herself onto the couch.

"You said yourself he's a terrible human."

"Yeah, but it doesn't mean I want him to die. And how are we going to get all the way across town without getting caught?"

"We'll be driving toward the hospital, right? So, if we get pulled over, we'll just say you're sick, and we're on our way there. No problem."

Lindsay circles her palm with her finger. "I don't know. That could work, but I still don't feel right about infecting this Nick guy."

I don't want to pressure her, but this might be the only chance we have of finding someone horrible enough to infect.

She grimaces, leans her head back, and rubs her temples. Her skin is pale, eyes hollow. "These jeans are murder on this rash, by the way." The words come out tired. She rubs furiously at her chest, legs, arms, and neck. "Oh my god." She groans. "This itching. This is the worst."

"Let's go." I help her up from the couch.

I get Lindsay into the car and send Nick a message:

```
On our way.
```

"Fuck." Lindsay groans, contorting her body to find comfort. "I don't wish this shit on anyone." Wet handprints darken her jeans. It reminds me of a Kindergartener's art project. "God damn this shit." She's sworn more in the twenty minutes we've been driving than the entire time I've known her.

Rippling gray clouds compound the eeriness of the empty streets. The world sleeps, and we're living a nightmare. We're a few minutes late, and I don't want Nick to leave if we're not there right away. I push hard on the accelerator. We're screwed either way if we get pulled over.

We approach the crest of a hill.

I glance in the rearview mirror.

A black car.

Fifty yards behind us.

"Shit."

"Hmm?"

"Uh, there's another car. Following us."

Lindsay maneuvers to see in the passenger-side mirror. "Shit. It's them."

I'm going seventy-four, but the black car is gaining on us.

Lindsay squeezes the sides of her head. "Ugh. I just want to die. I can't handle it."

"Hold tight. We'll figure something out." I signal as though I'm getting onto the highway.

The black car is only twenty feet behind us now.

I veer left on the ramp.

It follows.

I pull to the right just before the road divides.

Lindsay moans.

The black car follows.

Damn it.

"How far away are we?" Lindsay asks.

"Couple minutes. But I can't stop with this asshole tailing us." I glance in the mirror. We've put some distance between us and them. Good.

The black car turns.

"I think they left."

"Really?"

"Yeah, they just tur—"

I freeze with the flash of red and blue lights behind me. A lump sinks from my throat into my gut. "Oh, shit."

I slowly pull alongside the curb in front of a shuttered electronics store.

Lindsay curls into herself on the seat. Her face goes vacant.

I gather my license, registration, and insurance card, set everything on my lap, and place my hands on the steering wheel—ten and two. In the mirror, I watch the officer approach. He looks like a taller Kevin Hart, but with receding hair and a thick mustache. He's wearing baby purple surgical gloves and long sleeves. He stops behind my truck and speaks into the radio on his shoulder, then approaches my door. "You have a good reason to be out right now?" he asks.

"My...girlfriend is sick. I'm taking her to the hospital."

The officer leans over to peek around me.

His face twists in confusion. "Lindsay?"

"Ron?"

"What the hell are you doing out?" Ron's focus toggles between Lindsay and me. "You should have called an ambulance." He scowls at me. "You had to be going over ninety."

I can almost feel his glare boring holes in my face. "I'm sorry, sir. I just wanted to get her there as quickly as possible."

Ron looks at Lindsay. "You okay, kiddo?"

She shakes her head.

"What's the matter?"

Before she can respond, I say, "We think it's a relapse of the Grim Fever."

"Son of a...okay. I'm going to escort you the rest of the way."

That's not what we need right now.

"Oh, we're close," I say. "You don't need to do that."

His mustache stretches as he frowns. "Don't tell me what I need to do."

I can't keep arguing with him. "There was another car back there. It was behind us. Black sedan."

Ron scrunches his brows.

Lindsay nods. "Yeah, it turned just before you pulled us over. That's why Chad was driving so fast; we thought they were chasing us."

He looks to his right. Then back to me. "You get her there in one piece, you hear me? I don't care if there's no traffic, you keep it under the speed limit."

The tension in my chest eases. "I will. Thank you."

Ron leans into the window. "Lindsay, you let Kristin know what's going on, okay?"

"I will." She forces a weak smile.

"Take care, kiddo." Ron goes back into his car.

Lindsay grabs my wrist. Her hand feels like a microwaved fish slathered in butter. "Hurry up. I feel like I'm going to explode."

Ron's tires screech as he u-turns.

I head forward, watching his taillights shrink in the mirror. "We'll be there in just a couple minutes."

Two rights and a left later, I see the storefront. A block ahead, Nick's blue Jeep pulls into the lot behind the hardware store. I speed through the intersection. "That's Ni—"

The deafening impact of metal on metal jolts me.

My skull slams into the side window, glass shards pelt my face.

My brain whirls. I taste blood.

Somewhere close, a car peels out, tires shriek like a banshee.

A blue blur vaporizes before me.

I check Lindsay. Her head is slung to the side.

"Lindsay? You okay?" Through her shattered window, I see the roof of the black car.

It reverses. The driver's face appears.

I meet eyes with McNulty.

He sneers and opens the car door.

I pull the handle and push, but the door doesn't budge. I throw my shoulder into it. Nothing. It's jammed against a short retaining wall.

Lindsay groans. "What happened?" She's dazed.

"McNulty T-boned us."

Footsteps clunk closer to us through broken glass.

McNulty is at Lindsay's door, wrestling to open it. The damage from the collision compacted the metal, rendering the door useless. McNulty reaches inside the truck to release Lindsay's seatbelt. I grab his hand, but he swipes it away and clicks the button. In a swift motion, he wraps his arms around her and pulls.

Lindsay screams.

I lunge for them, but my seatbelt restrains me. I unbuckle, but McNulty already has her out.

I undo my seatbelt and scramble across the truck's seat.

Broken glass slices through my hands as I grab the window frame and pull myself out.

"Stop." McNulty aims his gun at me, squeezing Lindsay tight in his other arm

I freeze.

Lindsay struggles against his grasp, but she lacks the energy to put up much of a fight. Her feet slide on the asphalt. Her free arm flails limply.

"Don't make this difficult," McNulty says.

Lindsay swings her arm up and puts her hand on McNulty's.

Color floods back into her face, her eyes instantly full of vigor. She stomps his foot, slams a knee into his nuts, and lands an elbow to his wrist, knocking the gun free. She kicks the pistol under his car.

McNulty grunts. "Bitch."

Lindsay sprints to me. Behind her, McNulty dives to the ground and scrambles for his gun.

"We need to split up," I say as she reaches me. "Meet at the hospital lobby."

Lindsay's brows squeeze together, her eyes questioning and fearful, but she nods. "Okay."

"Go," I say.

She bolts and disappears around the building.

I raise my hands above my head and pace toward McNulty.

He aims his weapon at my chest. "Easy."

"I'm the one you want," I say. "I infected Lindsay. Leave her alone, and I'll go with you."

McNulty squints his right eye, presses his lips into a thread. "Why should I believe you?"

"Because it's the truth. I've had the virus for two years. Lindsay is the only other person I know that's survived."

"You're full of shit." He raises the gun level with my head.

I close my eyes. This is the end. I hope Lindsay gets away.

The gunshot provokes an involuntary jerk, and I fall to the ground.

"Holy shit," a voice calls out. A man, but not McNulty.

I open my eyes.

Feel my chest.

There's no blood.

No bullet hole.

I stand, draw my eyes to McNulty. He lies on his side, a gaping red hole in his chest. I have to look away.

Ron stands behind McNulty's car, gun drawn. "You okay,

Chad?"

"Yeah. I'm—"

Pop pop pop.

Ron collapses in a heap behind the sedan, a red mist lingers in the air.

Dr. Choi creeps out of a small recess between the buildings. She holds a gun in one hand, pointed at me.

Sweat drips down my back. I piss a little.

Choi gestures with the pistol toward the black car. "Please get in the car."

Her voice is soft. I'd even call it motherly in different circumstances.

She walks around the side of the vehicle. "I don't need you alive, but it would benefit us both if you cooperate."

My feet are anchored to the asphalt.

"You said you infected Lindsay Green?"

I nod.

"Interesting." She gestures again toward the car.

I inhale and take a step. And another.

Something will pluck me out of this awful dream, right?

Three more steps.

When I wake up, Leanne will be there to comfort me.

I'm ten feet away from Choi.

"Mr. Chaucer, we need to leave immediately. Get in the car. Now."

I take two steps. I'm at the front fender, directly across from her, the smashed hood of the car between us. "You're not from the CDC, are you?"

Choi smiles. She actually looks sweet, despite the pistol trained on me. "There is more going on here than you realize," she says. "Standing there looking stupid will do you no favors."

I look behind Choi.

She flinches but holds her gaze on me.

I look again and yell, "Lindsay, no!"

Choi spins.

I jump across the hood, sliding feet first, and slam my foot into Choi's arm.

The gun slams to the ground, along with Choi.

I kick the gun under my truck and kneel on Choi's chest, pinning one of her arms.

"Chad." Lindsay comes running from behind my truck. She sees Ron. "Oh my gosh, Ron!" She dashes to his side, touches his neck. "He's alive!"

I glare at Choi. "If he dies, you'll go away for a long time."

Choi is unmoved.

A sudden thwack to my ear drops me to the ground.

Everything sounds like I'm underwater.

Choi wriggles free.

"Lindsay," I try to yell, but I'm dazed. My ear is hot to the touch, my eyes refuse to focus. Did Choi knee me? I pull myself upright using the car for support.

Choi has vanished.

I spin in every direction. No sight of her.

I steady myself and wobble to Lindsay and Ron.

"He's bleeding a lot." Lindsay presses on his shoulder, blood oozes between her fingers.

I crouch and pluck the radio from his other shoulder. "Uh, hello? Officer down. Officer Ron," I look at his name badge, "Giggs. He's been shot."

The dispatcher snaps back through the speaker. "Who is this?"

"This is Chad Chaucer. I'm with Officer Giggs. Please send an ambulance to the parking lot of Graham's Hardware Supply, he's bleeding badly."

10

Lindsay and I enter the hospital lobby. Kristin springs from her chair and pulls Lindsay into a tight hug. The sisters detach and gaze at each other.

"What did the doctor say?" Lindsay says.

"He lost a ton of blood, but he's in the clear now. One bullet got him in the shoulder. Two hit his vest."

Lindsay sighs. "It was so scary." She wipes underneath her eyes. "All I could think of were you and the kids if —"

"I know." Kristin pulls her in for another hug and eyes me for an uncomfortable few seconds.

I offer a sympathetic smile.

Kristin waves me over.

"I'm glad Ron's going to be okay," I say.

Her lips tighten, and she almost smiles. She looks at Lindsay, then back at me. In a low tone, she says, "I don't know what you two were doing out today. I don't care, honestly. But it nearly got Ron killed." Her voice creaks. "But, you also saved his life." Her eyes flicker subtly before she tugs me by the elbow into their embrace.

I slip away to use the restroom while Lindsay and Kristin chat. I pass two uniformed officers and the detectives who took our statements at the scene.

They nod to me and continue their conversation. "Any idea where the nine-one-one call came from?" one of the uniformed officers asks.

"No idea."

I wondered that myself. Nick must have called nine-one-one before he took off. Makes me regret that we were there to infect Nick. If Ron hadn't arrived when he did, I'd be lying in a refrigerated drawer right now. I duck into the alcove for the restrooms and grab the men's room door handle.

"We still don't have a confirmed ID on the deceased," says the female detective.

I let go of the handle and lean against the wall to eavesdrop.

One of the officers says, "Really?"

"Yep. The witness gave the name Alex McNulty, but so far, nothing has come up. There are no Alex McNultys at the CDC. Need to wait on dental records."

The male detective says, "This case has a lot of open threads. Only one witness saw the female, the one that shot Giggs. Found the gun underneath the truck, but we have nothing on the woman."

"This case is already giving me an ulcer," says the female detective.

"Why would two people impersonate CDC officials?" an officer asks.

"You figure that out," says the male detective, "you let me know." He laughs, and the others join in.

I return to the waiting area. Lindsay beams a smile at me and pats the seat next to her.

I sit. "Where's Kristin?"

She gestures toward a group of uniformed officers circled

around Kristin. "She's talking to some of Ron's work buddies."

"How are you doing?" I ask.

She smiles so big that her teeth glow. "I'm good. Really good. Except, there's one thing that's been bothering me."

I cock my head. "What?"

"You told me we needed to split up and run."

"Yeah?"

"You didn't run."

"No. I didn't run."

"Were you planning to give yourself up to McNulty?"

"I wasn't planning anything. I just wanted you to get away from there."

Lindsay slow-blinks, bites her lower lip, and her eyes narrow. She grabs my hand and slides her fingers between mine, her skin cool and soft. "Thank you," she says and rests her head on my shoulder.

A culmination of repressed feelings explodes. I blink away tears and rest my head on Lindsay's. There are too many questions to answer, infinite unknowns on the horizon. But for the first time in two years, give or take a month, I put someone else's needs before mine.

I'm going to hold onto this moment for however long it lasts.

PART II

11

"You're killing me, Chad." Lindsay opens the cupboard and swings her head back. "Do you realize how selfish you sound?" She yanks a glass off the shelf and slams the cabinet door.

So I don't want to spend my life in prison for killing dozens of people. It's not selfishness; it's self-preservation.

Lindsay fills her glass with water and chugs it. "You've seen the treatment work for me." She wipes her mouth with the back of her hand. "I don't get why you wouldn't want the same for yourself. The lockdown is over, but you're still going to infect people. Another huge outbreak could happen again."

I belly up to the kitchen island opposite Lindsay. "I want the treatment. And believe me, I don't want another outbreak. But how many times do I have to say it? If I go to the doctor, they can trace all the infections at the prison back to me." The words come out defensively; that won't win her over. I move my coffee mug aside and lean forward on the island. "Sorry." I smile and reach across the counter to take her hand, but she turns around and sets her glass in the sink.

This morning marks the sixth time we've argued about this in the past two months, ever since the news reported on her being the only known survivor of Grim Fever. A week after that, she started receiving a combination of antiviral medications and steroids that help lessen the frequency and intensity of her symptoms. She's still infectious during the flare-ups, but she doesn't feel like she'll die every time a fever spikes or a purple rash blossoms. But she's wrong to think I can go to the doctor and get the treatment with no problems.

Her doctors used detectives from the Spokane Police Department to conduct contact tracing, and they tracked down every single person she came into contact with. They'd link me to the outbreak at the prison in no time. As much as I want the treatment to stop living from fever to fever, it's unattainable for me. My past is littered with the corpses of people I infected.

Lindsay stands at the sink, her back to me. Motionless. Silent.

Outside, storm clouds grumble, and the raindrops against the window sound heavier.

"Linds," I say. "Maybe I am being selfish. But do you want me to go to prison?"

She huffs. "Maybe you deserve to."

The words pierce like a bayonet. "Ouch."

Lindsay turns, her eyes moist with emotion. "I can't do this anymore."

"Do what?" I ask, but I know what she means.

She flicks her hand at me. "This. Us."

"No. I—"

"I won't tell anyone what you've done, Chad. I promise. But I can't be with you anymore."

A chill sweeps through my chest like I've inhaled an arctic mist. "Wait. We can figure some—"

"No." She glares at me, lips tight against her teeth. "I don't want to figure something out. We came together under weird circumstances, and we might have had a special bond because of that, but I will not put myself through the same fight over and over again with the same outcome."

My legs wobble. "Please." It sounds like a question.

"I care about you," Lindsay says. "But we can't..." She lets the words evaporate and shuffles out of the kitchen.

My body is unanchored, like I'm floating aimlessly in the middle of the Pacific. I can't lose Lindsay. She's the only person on the planet who understands me and what I've gone through. The only person I trust.

I've tried to convince her that the prison is still a suitable place for me to spread the illness; I have a more selective process, targeting the prisoners who have recently come into contact with outside visitors to give the illusion of external infection sources. It's not perfect, but it's sustainable. But our arguments have all ended the same way, with a promise to consider going to her doctor. Things go back to semi-normal for a while, only for us to fall back into the same fight a week later. Well, I have thought it over, and I'm not going to the damn doctor.

The toilet flushes. Seconds later, the bedroom door slams shut.

I stare into the hallway. The energy of our relationship has changed. Or maybe it's disappeared. Whatever it is, Lindsay feels it too. My feet move toward the bedroom before I make my mind up about what to do or what to say.

Wind and rain beat against the windows and roof. Everything is a varying shade of gray. I lumber to my room, psyching myself up to knock and ask if I can come in. I listen to Lindsay's footsteps scuff on the wood floor, back and forth between the bed and the closet. I finally muster some courage and raise my hand to knock, but she opens the door before my knuckles strike the wood. She gasps, her eyes spring wide open, and she almost falls backward. The strap of her bloated gym bag slides down her arm and knocks the plastic grocery bag in her hand to the floor, spilling her hairbrush and various toiletries.

"You're leaving?" I kneel to pick up her things, but she swoops down and swats my hand away.

She collects the items and stands upright. I expect anger or sorrow, but her face is blank. No emotion. She makes eye contact for half a second, then averts her focus and shoulders her way past me.

"Lindsay."

She strides to the front door.

I follow. "Wait. Please."

She opens the door and pauses, her hand still on the knob. She breathes in. I expect her to turn around and say something. But she walks out into the downpour and slams the door behind her, rattling the windows.

I stare at the doorknob, processing the finality of her exit. Hoping the door will open and she'll come back in. She's more or less lived with me for the past month. Are we really at the point of no return?

I should run after her.

Make promises.

Hold her.

Kiss her.

Have the same fight with her again in a few days after the polish of reconciliation wears away.

A few days ago, Lindsay said we keep circling around the same argument with the same predictable outcome, that we're two opposing forces unwilling to compromise. I understand why she wants me to do the right thing—her words, not mine—but I can't risk life in prison. I've seen first-hand what long-term prison sentences do to ordinary people. It demolishes them, cracks their foundation, steals any sense of morality. They're on edge every second of every day, bracing for an attack. Not to mention I'd have a bright red target on my back, given my profession.

I won't chase her, despite a powerful impulse to fling the door open and stop her from leaving.

I thought I would do anything for Lindsay, but I guess she's right. I am selfish.

Raindrops bounce like marbles off the roof of Lindsay's green Subaru. She was talking on her phone when she first got in the car but ended the call and still hasn't left. Her hands grip the wheel, eyes focused straight ahead. Every few seconds, her shoulders quake with sobs. She's been sitting there for at least five minutes. Maybe she's having second thoughts, or she's waiting out the storm that's drenching the street. Whatever the reason, I feel like a creep watching her through the window.

I go to the kitchen and pour the last dregs from the coffee pot into my mug. Only half a cup, but it'll do. I grab an old Stephen King novel I'd always intended to read and sit at the table. Rolling thunder drones in the distance. I open the book but can't make sense of the words. My mind isn't into it, my thoughts wandering to all the what-ifs with Lindsay.

Before we met, I'd been alone for two years. I had never considered a romantic relationship with anyone since Leanne died. But Lindsay survived Grim Fever after I accidentally infected her, and together, had some extraordinary experiences. We attended an anti-government group's rally so I could infect their leader, and we survived the terror of the two fake CDC agents who tracked Lindsay down. The events created a bond between us. We have a magnetic connection.

Had a magnetic connection.

Worldwide panic has dwindled with the discovery of effective treatments. SVE-1 is no longer the monster it once was, and that's partly why I feel justified in continuing to spread it at the prison. That's the wedge between Lindsay and me. Hell, more people die from drug overdoses than Grim Fever these days, especially on the res —

Oh, shit.

I'm so stupid. So caught up in my world that I never once considered Lindsay's family on the reservation, where meth overdoses have killed dozens this year. She's not only worried about me infecting more people; she has her family's safety on her mind. And it never occurred to me to ask her about it, to offer her the support she needs.

I don't deserve her.

My phone rings. I hope it's Lindsay calling, even though it's not her ringtone. I yank the cell out of my pocket. Unknown caller. Disappointment smothers me like a weighted blanket. I mute the ring, slide the phone back into my pocket but stop half-way and pull it back out. I need to tell her I'm sorry. Even if we don't get back together, she deserves an apology at the very least. I wonder if she's still out there. Better to do this kind of thing in person.

I jog to the front door. A deafening crack judders the windows, then a blinding flash brightens everything outside for a fraction of a second. My heart pumps, limbs fired up with adrenaline. I suck in a deep breath and calm myself, then peek out the window.

Lindsay's car is still there.

And she's running up the walkway toward the house.

I swing open the door.

She stops at the welcome mat, phone clutched at her side, clothes saturated. Soggy strands of hair cling to her face. Her eyes are red, her lips pressed into a thin line.

"You okay?" I ask.

"Frank…my cousin." She struggles to catch her breath. "He died last night. Overdose."

"Oh, no." My hand involuntarily covers my mouth. "I'm so sorry. Come inside."

She looks past me, inside the foyer, then focuses on me with a hard gaze. "Okay." She wipes the tears and raindrops from her face. "But only because I need to show you something."

"All right." I step aside, giving her space to enter.

She heads for the kitchen while I snatch a towel from the hall closet.

Lindsay sits and places her phone on the table. She stares at the towel in her hands. I've never seen her this shaken, even in the crazy situations we've found ourselves in. Her eyes show sadness, but her steel-trap jaw and death-grip on the towel scream anger. She looks across the table at me, then immediately drops her gaze to her phone. She clears her throat.

"I don't know…" She fights back tears, her wavering voice only a notch above a whisper. She sniffles, then continues, "Monica, Frank's sister, said someone has been delivering loads of meth straight onto the reservation. It started about four months ago." She squeezes the towel, her knuckles pale with tension. "Frank was clean for almost a year but began using again when these deliveries started coming."

I nod, unsure of what to say.

"Monica went to the police last week with a picture she took of the guys dropping off the meth. But they said without a license plate number or the identities of the men, they couldn't do anything. I asked her to send me the picture."

Lindsay swipes the screen on her phone and turns it toward me.

In the photo, two white men stand at the lowered tailgate of a red pickup truck parked amidst a cluster of pine trees. The men appear to be removing a cardboard box from the bed of the truck.

"Tough to kick an addiction when it shows up on your doorstep," I say.

"Look who's driving the truck."

I didn't notice the man behind the wheel.

Oh shit.

I jerk my head up. "When did Monica take this picture?"

"Eight days ago."

"How? That's impossible."

Lindsay shrugs. "I survived."

I glance again at the picture and see the face of a man who should be dead. I infected Wade Linford over two months ago. And yet, here he is. Alive and well, hand-delivering the drugs that killed Lindsay's cousin.

12

Rain pelts the kitchen windows, the sky almost night-dark. Thunder booms, a flashbulb sparks the sky, and the lights inside flicker.

I'm not entirely sure why Lindsay came back, but I'm glad she did. I have to be careful not to give her reason to leave. As much as I want to talk about how the hell Wade Linford is still alive, I have to focus on her needs right now. Be supportive, like I should have been all along.

"Were you and Frank close?" I ask.

Lindsay dabs underneath her nose with the towel. "When we were kids. Frank, Monica, Kristin, and me would have sleepovers just about every other weekend. They'd come stay with us for a week or two every summer. Monica is a year younger than me, and Frank and Kristin are—were—the same age, so they picked on me and Monica, but it was all in fun." A half-smile perks up in the corner of her mouth.

Lindsay's sister barely speaks to me, but they have a close relationship. "Does Kristin know about Frank?"

"Yeah. She's torn apart." Her voice quivers.

"I'll make you some lavender tea."

Lindsay nods.

I turn on the stove and ready the kettle. "Tell me about Frank. What was he like?"

"He was quiet but funny in a sneaky way. He'd whisper a joke to me in the back of the car. I'd giggle like crazy, and my mom or uncle, whoever was driving, would always get mad because I was so loud. Frank knew how to get me going."

"He sounds like a great guy."

"He was a good kid. But he got in a lot of trouble in high school. Stealing, smoking weed, stuff like that. He dropped out after his sophomore year. Got into the heavy drugs shortly after that, but he cleaned up when his wife left him."

I set the teacup in front of Lindsay along with a bowl of raw almonds, her favorite snack.

"Thank you." She blows away the steam and takes a sip. "Frank wanted to be there for his kids. He has a fourteen-year-old daughter and two boys still in diapers. He got sober through a program on the reservation. He was doing so well…"

"Where will the kids go?"

She sniffles. "Monica said she'll take them in."

"Do you talk to Monica often?"

"I do. She got me the gig teaching technology to the kids on the reservation."

Lindsay told me that before. I should have remembered.

"She called me," Lindsay says, "but she was crying so hard she couldn't get the words out, so she had to tell me about Frank through a text message." She crunches on a handful of almonds, losing herself in thought.

I don't dare interrupt her.

A few minutes pass without her saying a word. I open my mouth to ask another question about Frank, but she leans her elbows on the table, an intense rigidness across her face.

"I'm not sure what feeling is stronger," she says, "Sadness about losing Frank or hatred for Wade Linford."

"They go together, don't they?"

She nods. "I've never been a vengeful person. But I want to see that bastard pay for this. Not just for Frank, but for all the people he's killing with that poison."

"He's a cockroach. You think he's dead, but there he is, crawling out from under the rubble."

"Well, someone needs to smash him with a boot."

This is a side of Lindsay I've never seen. Her feelings are justifiable, but it's such a surprise coming from her.

"I wonder if there's anyone Ron can call." Lindsay's cop brother-in-law saved my life and nearly lost his doing so. "I'm sure there are jurisdictional issues, but the Spokane police department must have contacts on the reservation."

Lindsay shrugs. "I'm sure Kristin will tell him." She folds her arms across her chest. Her eyes go steely. "An investigation will take forever. How many more tribal members are going to die between now and then?"

I don't like where she's going with this.

"I want to track that son-of-a-bitch down myself."

"Let's just give the situation time to simmer before we—"

"No, Chad." She looks up at me without lifting her head. Death glare.

"Can I use your laptop?" she asks through gritted teeth.

I grab my laptop from the living room and set it in front of her. She types and clicks for a few seconds, then frowns. "The FATE Facebook group is private now."

FATE, Freedom Against Tyrannical Establishments, is Wade's anti-government group that held a protest a few months ago. We looked it up on their Facebook group to find the time and location.

"I guess they're being more careful after the violence broke out at their last rally."

Lindsay cocks her head to the side. "Are you kidding? They welcomed the violence. It was free advertising for their," she does air-quotes, "movement." She taps at the keyboard again. "I'm going to make a fake profile and join."

I'm as curious as her to see what they're up to, but we can't go too far with this. Not after the ruckus last time that got me injured and Lindsay nearly arrested. I watch Lindsay work with a nervous bubble inflating in my gut.

"How does this sound?" she says. "Jim Toole, relocated to Spokane from Coeur d'Alene, Idaho. Contractor, divorced, Patriot, Second Amendment advocate, God and Country."

"Sounds legit. But what if they check your previous posts? Won't they know it's a bogus account?"

"If they ask, I'll say my account was closed for inflammatory posts, so I had to create a new one."

"Jeez, have you done this before?"

She smirks.

Several minutes and hundreds of keystrokes later, Lindsay stands up. "It's done. Jim Toole just requested membership to FATE's private group." She turns the laptop screen toward me.

Jim's avatar is an illustration of a bald eagle clutching a rifle in its talons.

"Nice. What now?"

"We wait until an admin approves or denies Jim's request."

"All right. I'm hungry. Do you want some—"

A crack of thunder booms so loud I could swear it came from inside my skull. A flare of brilliant white light outside is followed by every light in the house going dark.

The rain is a steady drizzle. Dark gray hues coat everything like the earliest moments of the day before the dawn sun creeps over the horizon. The computer screen illuminates Lindsay's face, her eyebrows scrunched together as she reads. She hasn't spoken a word since the power went out.

"What?" she asks, catching me mid-stare.

"Nothing. Just wondering when they'll accept the request." I look away.

I gaze out the window and reflect on Wade and realize two of the last four people I've infected have survived. The two inmates are dead, but Lindsay and Wade are still alive. I thought Lindsay made it because we got into the hospital early. And because she's a fighter. But I keep tripping over my thoughts, stumped that Wade Linford is still breathing.

The virus must be mutating. The time between symptom outbreaks used to be a consistent four weeks, but lately, it's been sporadic—eight days after infecting Lindsay, five weeks after Wade, then only three weeks after that. It's wreaking havoc on my schedule.

"I just got a message," Lindsay says. "Dwight Basker wants to know why I'm interested in joining the FATE movement. Or, rather, why Jim Toole is interested." She looks at me over the computer.

"What are you going to say?"

She speaks as she types. "I want to associate with like minded patriots."

"I like it."

She taps a key and stares at the screen.

I stand up and walk around the table to see the screen. An icon of three blinking dots appears. Ten seconds later, the reply comes through.

    Welcome abroad!

"I guess that means we're in," Lindsay says.

"Or we're being sent to another country," I say.

Lindsay rolls her eyes and sighs. She clicks out of the messaging app and opens the FATE group page. She scrolls through the posts. Most are shared memes about tyranny and various videos that appear to be shot from cell phone cameras. She scrolls back to the top, where a pinned post reads:

```
Attention Patriots! This week's meeting
is still on! Newly added Patriots,
click HERE for the location.
```

Lindsay clicks the link, which opens a Google map location. "This is the middle of nowhere," she says.

"Zoom out a bit."

She does, and the location pin lies about twenty-five miles west of Spokane.

"Huh," Lindsay says. "That's just about half-way between here and the reservation."

She zooms in as far as Google allows. The meeting place is between three rectangular buildings, the property surrounded by trees.

"Is that residential?" I ask.

"Maybe. It's pretty far from any of the major roads. Or any other properties. And those buildings don't look like houses."

I point to the screen. "This one looks like a garage. Three cars parked next to it."

Lindsay points to the biggest building. "Think this is where they make their meth?"

"That's my guess."

Lindsay goes back to the Facebook page and scrolls to the Upcoming Events section. "The meeting is tomorrow at six p.m." She looks up at me, her jaw set and her eyes unwavering.

"I'm going."

I don't want to argue with her, but that's insane. What does she hope to accomplish? Wade's dangerous, and if FATE meets where he deals his drugs, that's even more dangerous.

"What?"

"I…what do you mean, what?"

"Your face. You look like you're about to say, 'That's a bad idea, Lindsay.'"

"Well, that is a bad idea, Lindsay."

She shakes her head and stands up.

"Where are you going?"

"The bathroom. Is that okay?"

"Oh. Of course."

She stomps past me and out of the kitchen.

I can't let her go to that meeting, but it's not my place to tell her what to do. Maybe I can reason with her.

The toilet flushes and the sinks runs for a few seconds. I wait for Lindsay to come back to the kitchen, but from the foyer, she says, "I'm leaving."

"Wait!" I dash around the corner to the foyer.

Lindsay holds her hand on the doorknob and raises a disinterested eyebrow. "What?"

"You can't…I mean, it's not safe to go there. Those guys are lunatics."

"I'm not going there to pick a fight, Chad. I'm just going to see what they're up to. If there's anything I can give to Ron to speed up an investigation."

"If they catch you…"

"They won't catch me."

"I hate the idea of you going there."

"Why? Because I'm a helpless woman?"

"No, I've seen you kick guys' asses. It's not that. I just don't think Wade is above extreme violence if he finds someone sniffing around. And who knows if everyone in his stupid group is in on the drug operation."

"I'm going." She turns the knob and swings the door open. The rain has let up, but the world is still gray.

"Are you going to tell them you're Jim Toole?"

Lindsay stops. She sighs and looks over her shoulder. "Come with me."

Damn it, that backfired. "Lindsay…"

"I am going. With or without you. I'll come up with some bullshit story if you don't." She turns and hustles toward her car.

I hate this.

"Fine. But only to look around, all right? We're not freaking CIA agents."

"I'll pick you up at five-fifteen."

"All right." I shake my head. This is not going to end well, but I know she means it when she says she'll go with or without me.

Lindsay gives a little nod and opens the car door.

"Hey."

She stops and looks over the car at me.

"I'll drive. A Subaru might look a little out of place."

13

A fight broke out at the prison today. Not a riot but a handful of inmates who acted out on their differing views over what must have been quite an important topic. My shoulder, still not a hundred percent from an incident a few months ago, absorbed the brunt of the impact with the cement floor. I had an inmate restrained, but an acquaintance of his thought it would be fun to shove the two of us. I landed shoulder-first on my right side, and the inmate tumbled on top of me. I've had ice on the shoulder since I got home an hour ago, but it's still throbbing like there's a rave going on inside my AC joint.

My phone buzzes. I expect Lindsay since she'll be here in half an hour to pick me up for this evening's FATE meeting, but it's another unknown number. My head swims in anxiety. I don't think going to this meeting will be anything but negative. She says she only wants to see what it's about, won't do anything but observe. I want to believe her, but I've had a twitchy stomach all day, and it's gotten worse since I've been home from work.

Water sloshes outside as a car drives past. I peek out the

kitchen window — still gray and wet, with no sign of letting up.

My phone buzzes again. It's Lindsay this time. "Hello?"

"You don't have to come," she says, monotone.

"I want to."

"No, you don't."

"Well, it's not the most romantic date, but it'll do."

Silence.

Chad, you dummy.

Lindsay coughs.

"Sorry." I clear my throat. "Seriously, I want to go with you." I feel the need to protect her, but Lindsay is one person who does not need protecting. Hell, she's more likely to save me if things go south. "I want to help you get justice for Frank."

She blows out a stream of air. "All right. I'm on my way."

The sky rumbles just as the call ends. Fitting.

I can't extend my right arm without my shoulder screaming in fiery agony, so I hold the wheel one-handed. Lindsay leans against the passenger door, elbow on the armrest. We're both wearing the same outfits we wore to the FATE protest — me in a camouflage shirt and a red USA trucker hat, Lindsay in Wranglers and a red USA t-shirt. She hasn't spoken since we left my house, and the uncomfortable silence in the truck and the choruses of guilt in my mind remind me of our ride to the hospital when I first infected her.

After several empty minutes pass, Lindsay stirs. "Just because we're doing this doesn't mean we're getting back together. Got it?"

Dagger. In. The. Heart.

"I know."

She stretches her legs in front of her, adjusting her jeans. "These things are so tight."

I open my mouth to say something about how good they look on her but think better of it and bite my tongue. The GPS guides us through farmland thirty minutes outside of the city. Small houses dot the landscape, most of them at least a mile from the nearest neighbor. Mailboxes on the road mark the start of long driveways that lead to modest homes surrounded by massive property lots. The area is remote but not desolate.

Sometimes I think it would be wonderful to live outside of town, detached from society. Before, with Leanne, I would have never dreamed of living outside of a big city. Pittsburgh had every amenity we could ever need. Bars, restaurants, shops. Places we would meet up with friends. But that life is gone, replaced with a lonely existence.

I deserve to be alone.

"It's really soggy out here," Lindsay says, breaking me from my pitiful thoughts.

The ground is saturated. There's nothing but mud, soaked grass, and puddles in every direction. I hope whatever turnoff we need to take is more road and less muck.

"Do you ever think about McNulty and Choi?" Lindsay asks.

"Yeah. I wonder every day if Choi—or whatever her name is—will pop up out of nowhere." Choi shot Lindsay's brother-in-law cop in the shoulder seconds after he saved my life. The doctors said he was lucky the bullet struck where it did. He lost some blood, but there was no lasting damage. "Has Ron said anything about them?"

"Nope. Choi vanished like a ghost. He hasn't heard anything back on McNulty, and he doubts he ever will."

"It's freaky. I'm kind of scared to find out who they're working for and why they used the CDC as their cover."

"Wherever they're from, I want no part in it."

I exhale like I'm blowing out birthday candles. "Have you

been getting calls from an unknown number?"

"No. Why? Have you?"

"Yeah."

"Have you answered?"

"No. I keep thinking it'll be Choi." I let out a pathetic laugh. "It's probably a telemarketer or something."

"Yeah." Lindsay doesn't elaborate any further.

The GPS pings, showing our next turn. I slow the truck and scan for the road, but I can't see it.

"There it is—was," Lindsay says.

I hit the brakes, then back up. The driveway is hidden among a grouping of trees. And it's unpaved. Great. I turn onto the road, and my tires churn through the thick mud chowder.

"For the record," Lindsay says, "my Subaru would make it through this."

She doesn't say it jokingly, but I grin anyway.

We chunk our way along the muddy road toward a cluster of structures and pull into a circular gravel lot centered between the buildings. No other vehicles are around except for a rusty tractor and a seventies-era pickup truck with missing wheels and doors. The first building looks like a portable trailer, similar to what would house a foreman's office at a construction site. Next to that lies a rectangular building that resembles a barn with a green tin roof and sliding barn doors. Adjacent to that building sits a small cinderblock structure with a matching green roof and a roll-up garage door big enough to drive my truck through.

"Where is everyone?" Lindsay says. She pulls out her phone. "Dang it."

"What?"

"I don't have any service out here."

I check my phone. No bars.

Lindsay slides her phone into her pocket. "I wonder if they

canceled the meeting because of the rain. I should have checked before we left." She leans her head back on the headrest and draws circles on her palm, her tic whenever she's anxious or in deep thought.

I turn the truck around.

"What are you doing?"

"Leaving."

"Wait. Let's check it out."

My gut twitches and electric pulses radiate on the back of my neck. "I don't know. I don't think these are the kind of people who would take snooping around their stuff lightly."

Lindsay opens the door and slides out of the truck.

I guess we're snooping around then.

I turn off the truck and get out. I glance down the long driveway. No one is coming, but my tension doesn't ease. I spin and examine the environment. Trees surround the entire property. The driveway is the only way in or out.

Lindsay walks up to the portable-office-looking building and peeks into the windows.

"What do you see?"

"Couches and some chairs. A desk. Looks like a couple of mini-refrigerators. Beer cans all over the floor."

I glance at the muddy road again. Empty.

Lindsay moves on to the largest structure. She tugs on one of the barn doors, but it doesn't budge. She walks around to the other side.

I walk around my truck and step into a puddle because that's my luck. Damn it.

Surrounded by trees, anything could happen at this site, which makes it the perfect spot for a militia to produce meth. I survey the largest building. It looks sturdy. And then I see something that knots my gut. Crap. "Lindsay, come here." I try to emphasize urgency without shouting.

She glares at me.

"Please. Come here."

She grunts and walks over to me.

"Don't look now, but there are cameras on that building." I check out the other two structures, but neither has visible surveillance. "Only that big one has cameras. There's probably something in there that's worth—"

"Drugs. That has to be where they make their meth."

"Yeah. So let's not mess around here anymore."

Lindsay rolls her eyes and shakes her head. She looks at the third structure—the garage. "One quick peek, then we can go." She shuttles off toward the building before I can protest.

I climb into the truck and get it started, then glance in the rear-view mirror. There's no one there, but the acid in my stomach churns anyway.

Lindsay disappears around the backside of the garage. She comes around the front and shakes a padlock attached to the roll-up door. She then drops to her hands and knees and peeks through a crack under the garage door. She stands, wipes her hands on her jeans, and comes back to the truck.

"Anything interesting?" I ask, turning the truck around.

"Looks like a mechanic's shop. There's a small door on the backside with a big metal bar across it."

"Perfect. I need an oil change."

Lindsay glares at me without a trace of humor and gets in the truck. The gravel crunches under the tires as we leave the property, and soon we're squelching through mud again. Between the thrumming pain in my shoulder and my cold, drenched sock, a hot shower and a bottle of beer sounds like the perfect remedy. I swerve to avoid a threatening puddle, and Lindsay gasps.

"You okay?" I ask.

"Yeah, just surprised me."

"Sorry it didn't work out. With the meeting, I mean."

Lindsay shrugs. "There'll be another one, I'm sure."

We come up to the paved road. I'm thankful we didn't get stuck in the goop.

"Wait," Lindsay says. "Turn right."

"Why?"

"Would you mind taking me to see Monica?"

"On the reservation?"

"Yeah. If you don't want to, that's fine. It's just—"

"No problem."

"Thank you."

I turn right and head toward the reservation. That hot shower will have to wait.

14

"Take a left up here," Lindsay says.

I turn onto the westward road just as the sun breaks out through the clouds. The white-hot sunlight contrasts with the iron-gray clouds and blinds me for a few seconds.

"You okay?" Lindsay must have noticed my pained squint.

"Yeah. Where to now?"

"Park in the lot on the left. Monica's in that building over there." She points to a building the size of a typical restaurant.

I park and lean out of the truck, forgetting that my shoulder is in no shape to be used for leverage. I grimace as sparks flare in the damaged joint. I suck in a breath and follow Lindsay toward the building.

"Monica runs a behavioral health class." She checks the time on her phone. "She should be out in a few minutes."

I nod and turn my attention to a group of teens playing basketball where a girl stands half a foot taller than all the boys. She grabs a rebound, dribbles through a series of defenders, and pulls up to sink a three-pointer. Elementary-aged kids play soccer on the field next to the parking lot. Squeals of delight emanate from the grassy area.

The ball trickles over to me. I pop it up with my foot, bounce it on alternating knees a few times, drop it to my foot and stall it, holding it balanced on my shoelaces six inches above the ground. I haven't handled a soccer ball in years, so I'm surprised that I've still got a decent touch. The kids ooh and ahh. I pop the ball up with a quick flick and kick it back to them. The smallest boy of the bunch collects the ball and stares at me, jaw wide open.

I smile, and the boy runs back to his friends. "Did you see that?"

"Come on, Messi," Lindsay says with a smirk. She leads us to a door on the side of the building. Inside, several tribal members congregate in a reception area. Most of the men eye me for a moment before granting me a gentle nod. The women smile, some say hello.

"In here," Lindsay says.

I follow her into a room lined with rows of chairs. A podium and a fold-out table sit at the front of the room where a woman in a maroon dress stacks papers on the table.

"Monny!" Lindsay runs to her cousin, and they squeeze each other into a gravitational hug.

"What are you doing here?" Monica asks.

"I wanted to come see you." Lindsay's voice sounds different somehow.

They hug again. When they pull apart, Monica looks at me, then back to Lindsay. "Is this Chad?" she whispers.

I suspect I wasn't meant to hear her.

Lindsay waves me over. "Yeah, this is Chad."

"Nice to meet you, Monica. I'm so sorry to hear about Frank."

A sad smile comes over her face. She bows her head and says, "Thank you."

"How are your mom and dad handling it?" Lindsay asks.

"Devastated. Dad actually came to the meeting tonight. I'm surprised you didn't see him out in the hall."

Lindsay frowns. "Oh, I missed him. I'm glad he came, though."

Monica twists her lips and grabs Lindsay's arm. "I'm happy to see you, Lin-Lin."

"Me too." Lindsay reaches out and squeezes Monica's hand.

Monica asks about Kristin. Then they talk about people I don't know, presumably other tribal members and family. Both sniffle and hold back tears, interrupted by the occasional shared giggle.

My head vibrates with an oncoming headache. It's probably from looking directly at the sun; my eyes still haven't adjusted. At least my sock is mostly dry. If only my shoulder would stop thumping internally.

I notice the break in the conversation a few beats after the last word.

Lindsay's face has gone stern. "Monny, was Frank into anything weird lately? Like…political stuff?"

Monica twists her face. "Why do you ask?"

"Just curious."

"It's funny you say that. He's been posting all sorts of anti-government things. Like memes and stuff."

I step closer, and Lindsay leans in. "How long has he been doing that?"

"A couple months. Maybe three or four?" Monica looks away, then back to Lindsay. "And you know what? David said he kept talking about the guys that were delivering the meth. Like, interested in them. I didn't think about that until just now."

"Does anyone around here know who those guys are?"

Monica shakes her head. "I don't know. Ask David or Nina.

They might know."

Lindsay gives me a look, but I can't tell what it means. She turns back to Monica. "I'll ask them. Thanks. It was good to see you, Monny. Take care."

"You too." Monica waves to me. "Nice to meet you, Chad."

Outside, Lindsay hurries toward the truck. The sun is out, and the clouds have broken up into clusters. My head now throbs in sync with my shoulder.

Lindsay stops at the truck. "Can we make one more stop? Please."

"Of course. Just tell me where to go."

I open the door and climb in one-handed, remembering my bum shoulder this time. I start the engine and scratch the sudden itch on my chest.

Oh, no. Not now.

My shoulder screams in agony if I try to scratch the rash with my right hand, and releasing my left hand's grip on the steering wheel isn't an option on these curvy roads. I try rubbing myself against the seatbelt, but it doesn't give me any relief. Lindsay assures me we're close. A relentless fiery itch engulfs my chest, and we can't arrive soon enough.

"Left at the mailbox," Lindsay says.

I turn, and we travel down a long tree-lined corridor. Wisps of sunlight flick through the trees, long shadows stretching across the road like gray fingers grabbing the earth. After a slight left turn, the trees open up into a small clearing. A modest white house with forest green trim stands in the middle of the opening. Beside the house sits a motorboat atop a trailer. Two lifted Chevy trucks are parked in front of the closed garage.

I shut off the engine and, as casually as possible, scratch my chest. "Should I wait in the truck?"

Lindsay scrunches her face. "No...you can come in. But David's always had a thing for me, so he might be a little stand-offish with you." She cocks a mischievous smile.

"Good to know. Should I be nervous?" I return a half-smile.

Lindsay waves it off. "No. He's a teddy bear. I messaged him to let him know we were coming, so he's expecting you."

"What is it you want to know from him?"

"He's Frank's best friend. He'll know if Frank was doing anything with Wade."

I ease out of the truck, and a thought stops me. What if David tries to shake my hand? I don't have the sweats yet, but I don't want to risk infecting him. I'll say I have a cold or something. Hopefully, Lindsay plays along or ignores the lie.

Lindsay knocks three times on the front door, then opens it and walks in. "David?"

"In here," a deep voice booms from around a corner.

Kids' toys litter the floor. Barbies, stuffed animals, Ninja Turtles, Nerf dart guns. I follow Lindsay into a living room. David, presumably, sits on an L-shaped sofa; two toddlers in pajamas lie asleep on his lap.

"Hey, Lin-Lin." He strokes one of the kid's hair, then looks at me. He tips his head back with a quick jerk. "Hey."

"Hi. I'm Chad. Nice to meet you."

He looks down at the sleeping children, then to Lindsay. "Let me put them to bed." In a swift motion, he stands and swoops each child into his arms with graceful ease. David passes me, and I'm overwhelmed at his stature—he's at least six-five and pushing three hundred pounds. The kids each lie their sleepy heads on his shoulders, and he carries them into the hallway.

Moments later, a door closes in the hall, and David comes back into the living room. He hugs Lindsay. She lets go, but he gives another squeeze before releasing her.

I stay back, hoping to avoid an awkward hand-shaking situation.

David steps toward the couch. "Have a seat."

Phew.

I sit at the end of the sofa. Lindsay sits perpendicular to David on the couch, their knees almost touching. "How are you doing?" she asks.

"Been better." He props his elbows on his legs, leans his chin onto his hands. "It's sad. Frankie was doing good. Laid off the drugs, even stopped drinking. Don't know what made him start doing it again."

Lindsay frowns and breathes in through her nose. "Was Frank doing anything weird? Like, meeting with anyone outside the res?"

David turns toward Lindsay and fixes on her with an intense gaze. "Yeah. How d'you know that?"

"Have you heard him talk about a guy named Wade? Or a group named FATE?"

David rubs his stubbly cheeks. "He was hanging out with some white dudes, but I don't know their names." David glances at me quickly, then back to Lindsay. "I never heard him say anything about any groups."

I sneak a chest scratch when he looks away.

"Was Frank into, like, anti-government stuff?"

"Yeah. He always was. Why?"

Lindsay squints briefly. "I think the guys that were selling him meth are also running a militia kind of thing."

David leans back into the couch. "I mean, I guess he was posting some pretty crazy things. Like, crazier than before."

Lindsay squeezes his knee. "Sorry, I know I'm throwing a bunch of questions at you."

He looks at her hand. "It's all right."

I lean forward. "You said he was hanging around the white guys. Was that here on the reservation or somewhere else?"

David shrugs. "Both. He tried to get me to go to drink some beers with them a few times, but I couldn't leave the kids."

The front door opens and shuts. David looks over his shoulder.

"Hey, Sabrina. Lin-Lin's here."

The tall teenage girl that was dominating the basketball court enters. She's taller in person than she looked before, at least five-eleven. She comes in and hugs Lindsay.

Lindsay looks up at her. "You've grown a foot since the last time I saw you."

Lindsay introduces me, and Sabrina disappears into the back hallway.

"Do you know where Frank was going to drink beers with those guys?" I ask.

David shakes his head. "Frankie said some dude has property on the county land between here and the city. They have parties and stuff there all the time, I guess."

Lindsay gives me an affirmative glance. "Thank you, David. It's good to see you."

"You too." David stands up, towering over Lindsay. He swallows her in a hug and says, "Don't be a stranger."

I walk past him. "Thanks, David. Sorry to hear about your friend."

His lips go into a straight line, and he nods once.

I climb into the truck. I'm dizzy and nervous about driving, but I back out and train my focus on the road.

We drive back through the tree tunnel and head toward Spokane. The sun is sinking behind the mountain horizon, casting an amber-hue over the landscape. On a straight road, I sneak a quick scratch of my itchy chest. The relief is short-lived but worth it.

Lindsay looks at her phone.

"David seems nice," I say.

Her eyes stay focused on the screen. "Yeah."

"His daughter is quite the basketball player."

"Mm-hmm."

This is going well.

I huff a quick breath. "Look, I'm sorry. If there's a way—"

"Stop. We're not getting back together. Thanks for helping me, but that doesn't mean I'm just going to forget everything and take you back."

Message received.

"Holy shit!" Her shout makes me jump.

"What?"

"Pull over and watch this."

I slow and pull to the side of the road.

Lindsay hands me her phone. "Press play."

She has the FATE Facebook page loaded. I play the video. It's a shaky phone recording of men in military-style gear hollering, drinking beer, and posing with AR-15 rifles. It's at the location Lindsay and I visited earlier today. The twenty-second video ends without fanfare.

"What did I miss?"

"Play it again and look in the background. Recognize anyone?"

I do. As the video pans the group, it captures a shot of several vehicles parked next to each other. I pause it. Clear as day—I don't know how I missed it the first time—is a blue Jeep Wrangler. Standing behind it is Nick Ansley, the drug-dealing correctional officer from my prison.

15

"Son-of-a-bitch." I pace in my kitchen. "That explains the meth ODs at the prison. Fucking Nick. I can't believe I didn't make the connection before."

Lindsay stands at the counter, gnawing on the inside of her cheek. Her puckered lips make her look like a gerbil nibbling on a seed. She checks her phone.

I consider going to the police to investigate the prison overdoses and the connection to Nick, but I don't want anyone snooping around the prison since I'm the link to the Grim Fever cases there. Of course Nick knows Wade—jerks of a feather and all that.

"Call him," Lindsay says.

"Nick?"

"No, the Pope." She glares at me.

"What the hell am I going to say? 'Hey, Nick, can you introduce me to Wade Linford so my…friend can confront him?'"

"I don't know, Chad. I don't know what we're doing here." It's not quite a shout, but it's close. She steps toward the foyer.

"I want justice for Frank and all the others that died because of Wade. I want that asshole to pay. But I don't know what I can do. Monica already went to the police. There's nothing they can do legally."

"What about cutting off the supply? Have the tribal police be on alert for Wade's truck."

"Maybe, but they're already stretched thin. They have a tiny budget as it is, and only a few officers. Did you see any police cars while we were there?"

"No. But it's worth a shot."

Lindsay shoots a death stare my way.

My shoulder is on fire, the fever is pummeling my brain, and the rash makes me want to tear my skin off. The last thing I want to do right now is argue.

I raise my hands, palms up. "What do you want to do, then?" I say it softly, masking the anger I'm feeling.

Lindsay shrugs. "I don't have a plan. Maybe we can find evidence of drugs on that property and take it to the county police."

"So, you want to go to the headquarters of a drug dealing, anti-government militia to find their drugs and report them to the police?" It sounds even more ridiculous out loud.

She crosses her arms and shifts her weight to one side. "Yes."

"And you're going with or without me, right?"

"I'm going without you. I can handle myself."

"Lindsay—"

"No. I'm not some princess who needs a bodyguard."

I want to let her go, wash my hands of our relationship. She doesn't need me to protect her. I should break whatever threads of our bond remain now. Quick and mostly painless.

Lindsay stomps out and slams the door.

Her tiles squeal.

I lower my head and close my eyes to resist the oncoming flood.

My phone sits screen-up on the coffee table next to the plate of untouched leftover chicken I reheated. I stare at the phone like it might get up and dance. Am I hoping Lindsay calls? Or am I psyching myself up to call her? She's done with me, and I don't blame her—we have irreconcilable differences—but she's about to walk into the mouth of a monster, and I let her go. I doubt she'd answer if I called.

I flip open my laptop. The headache blurs my vision and delays my focus, so I have to close one eye to see the screen. Lindsay's fake Jim Toole profile is still logged in. Curiosity takes over, and I scroll through the FATE video posts:

A group of men slam beers and throw their cans into a fire.

Three men shoot AR-15s at silhouette targets.

Wade, without his familiar scraggly beard, lectures a group of a dozen on the importance of fighting the government at all levels.

The video with Nick in the background.

The count of videos posted is endless, but there's nothing interesting about any of them. I'm bored, so I reach to close the laptop lid. I stop when I notice under the FATE title a line of text that reads 'Private group: 41 Members.' I click the tab to view all members. Wade Linford and Dwight Stone are listed as administrators. In the search bar labeled, 'Find a member,' I enter 'Nick Ansley.'

His smug face appears next to his name. I click his profile, which displays his posts to the group. His last entry was three weeks ago, but before that, he posted daily. Why did he stop?

I close the laptop and look at the plate on the coffee table. I poke the chicken breast. It's gone cold, and I question why I even prepared it.

My eyes track to the phone. Lindsay doesn't want my help, and when I take a step back and think about it, I don't have any reason to go after Wade the way she does.

I'm not going to get involved. This isn't my fight, and Lindsay doesn't need help. I'm going to live as if I never infected Lindsay. Never had feelings for her. Never wished we could be back together.

In what feels like an out-of-body experience, I reach for the phone and swipe open the lock screen. Without hesitation, I tap the recent calls, scroll down, and tap the number.

It rings four times.

"Hello?"

"Hey, Nick?"

"Uh…hey, Chad."

"Yeah. What's up, man?"

"Um, nothing. You know dispensaries are open again, right?"

I laugh, a little too forced. "I know." Damn. I didn't think this through. I've seen him at work a dozen times since I called him to buy marijuana gummies during the lockdown, so calling him like this is awkward. "I just, uh…do you remember when we were going to meet up a few months ago?"

"Yeah, bro. You got smashed by that dickhead in the black car. Crazy. What was that about?"

"I don't know. I guess the guy thought I was someone else, maybe. Anyway, did you call nine-one-one?"

"Yep. Then I bolted the hell out of there."

"Well, thanks for calling. It ended up saving our lives."

"No problem, man." A sound like a plastic wrapper crinkling comes over the line. "So, was that why you called?"

"Uh, yeah. I…can I buy you a beer?"

Silence.

"You know, as a 'thank you.'"

More crinkling. "All right," Nick says with a mouthful of food. "I never turn down free beer." He chews and smacks his lips. "You work tomorrow?"

I have to think about what day it is. "No, I'm off."

"Me too. Grimstone Brewery opens at noon."

I wait for more. He just chews. "All right. See you then."

I'm tempted to message Lindsay to let her know I called Nick. Instead, I focus my energy on coming up with a plan to convince Nick to get me proof that Wade Linford is selling meth on the reservation.

I'm glad Nick wanted to meet here. Grimstone is my favorite local brewery, and its riverside patio has an incredible waterfront view. Nick isn't here yet, so I seat myself at a table outside on the empty patio. The sun is bright, but puddles and damp umbrellas remind me of yesterday's rain. The sky is blue above, but clouds threaten in every direction, forming a gray halo around the sun.

I haven't come up with anything to get Nick talking about Wade and the meth operation, so I'll wing it and hope for an opening. The server greets me, and I ask for a glass of water and bread. The headache is at a tolerable throb. Fresh air seems to help. I just wish I had a remedy for this terrible itch. I try to put it out of my mind.

I finish half the bread in the basket and down two glasses before Nick saunters outside, scanning the empty patio. I wave him down, and he plops into a chair, causing too much ruckus for one person.

"Hey, man," he says.

"Hey. I was going to order food, too. It's my treat if you're hungry."

"Sweet. Money's been a little tight lately, so I'll take a free meal." He snatches a menu from the table and drums his fingers as he looks over it.

The server comes out and takes our orders—rib platter and an IPA for Nick, bacon burger and an imperial stout for me. Of course he'd order the most expensive entrée, but he provided me with an in—money trouble—so I ask, "You had a side-gig going, right?"

Nick sucks on his lower lip and eyes me like he's trying to figure out the meaning of an abstract sculpture.

Damn it. I jumped the gun.

Nick nabs a piece of bread and bites off a hunk. "Yeah. I had a little something going on." He grins like a cocky frat boy.

The server comes out and drops off our beers.

Nick takes a hefty gulp from his glass. "What are you getting at?" The overconfident smirk shifts into a sneer.

Shit. How do I play this? Do I act like I'm into the militia thing? Do I come right out and tell him about Lindsay's cousin and ask about Wade? I'm so screwed.

"Do you know Wade Linford?" No! The words slip out. I shouldn't have said anything. Oh, shit. I totally—

"Yeah. He's a piece of shit. How do you know him?" He says it more out of curiosity than suspicion.

I'm stunned by his reaction. "He, uh...sold meth to my girlfriend's cousin." Cue internal cringe.

Nick sits back in his chair and sips his beer. "Huh. So, are you like, hunting him down or something?"

"No. No, nothing like that. I just...I'd love to get something to take to the police. To shut him down, you know?"

Nick plucks the last piece of bread out of the basket and rips a chunk off. He pops it in his mouth. While chewing, he says, "He's not someone you fuck around with. Dude's got an army behind him. You mess with him, your gambling with your life."

"I'm not trying to start a fight. I just want to get something to take to the police."

Nick downs the half-full glass and slams it on the table. He leans forward onto his elbows. "Wade fucked me over. I wouldn't mind seeing him go down. I can take you to his place," he says, two notches above a whisper. "Where he makes his stuff."

I follow Nick to Wade's property, and the trip seems to go by faster than the previous one. Funny how travel time seems different when you're going somewhere you've been before.

He parks his Jeep in the gravel and waves me over. "Park on the other side, by that garage."

Nick stands in front of his Jeep, his phone at his side.

The ground is still soft from the rain, but the puddles have since dried up. I get out and walk toward Nick. I flick my head toward the big building. "What about those cameras?"

"Oh, don't worry about that. My buddy Mike is the only one that ever checks them. He's cool. Hey, I need to make a quick call, all right? Lady troubles." He taps his screen and puts the phone to his ear. "Hey, it's Nick … I know, but hear me out, okay…" He walks around the side of his truck and leans against the fender. I can't hear what he's saying. None of my business anyway.

I stroll toward the small building. The padlock on the garage door is enormous. I realize the door touches the ground now, closing the gap that Lindsay peeked through yesterday. Were these tire marks here then? I step closer. The mud in front of the garage is impacted. Someone must have pulled a vehicle into the garage. I hear Nick open his car door, but I'm too focused on the mud prints to care. I look around the sides of the building. There are no signs of anyone here.

Nick's voice gets louder. "What do you mean? … What woman? … Oh, shit. No way! … All right. Bye."

I spin around toward Nick.

He's pointing a handgun at me. He slides the phone into his pocket with his other hand.

"What is this, Nick?"

"Hands up. Go around to the back." He gestures with the gun.

"Nick...what are you doing?"

"It's not personal. You seem like a good dude. But Wade cut me out of his operation, and catching somebody snooping around his place will get me back in his good graces."

I step back. "You don't have to do this." He's standing between me and my truck now. I could probably run to the other side of the building, but it's a good fifty feet before the tree line. My legs go weak. Heart races. Sweat pours from my hands.

"Oh, I do need to do this. I need the money, man. My ex is making me pay a thousand a month for child support."

"There has to be another way. Help me get Wade arrested. We can find a way to get you money."

"Hmm." He tilts his head as if deep in thought. "Nope."

"Are you going to kill me? You don't think people at the prison are going to ask questions?"

"I'm not going to kill you, Chad. But I am going to lock you in this garage. Whatever happens after that isn't my problem."

"Nick—"

"Move!" He charges toward me with the pistol aimed at my

chest.

I raise my hands, but my right shoulder feels like it's being ripped out of the socket, so I put them in front of me. "Okay. Okay. I'm turning around, all right?" I slowly turn my back to him. The hairs on my neck stand at full salute. I can feel the eye of the gun staring at my exposed body.

"Wait. Take your keys, wallet, and phone out of your pockets."

I remove the items and set everything on the ground in front of the garage door.

"Go."

I walk around the side of the building. Slow steps. Left hand above my head, my right as high as the pain allows. Trickles of sweat gliding down my wrists and forearms. Not now. Unless...maybe I can infect Nick.

"Keep going," he says.

I stop at the door.

"Undo the latch."

I struggle to lift the two-inch solid metal bar between the excruciating pain in my shoulder and my moist hands.

"Come on," Nick says.

I finally get the bar lifted.

"Open the door and get inside."

I reach for the doorknob but halt.

"Get in."

How can I touch him? He's wearing short sleeves, but he's going to think I'm going for his gun. Sweat drips from my fingertips. I have to find a way to infect him.

That's it. I have to try to disarm him.

"Open the door."

I cautiously turn back toward him.

He's too far. I can't get to him before he'd shoot.

"Nick."

"Turn around. I don't want to kill you, but I will shoot your ass."

I extend my left hand. "Please."

"Open the fucking door." He bares his teeth, snarling like a rabid wolf.

My slim chance evaporated. I turn around, twist the knob, and push the door open.

There's an SUV inside. Green. Muddy tires.

Oh shit.

It's Lindsay's Subaru.

I hear shuffling footsteps, and then Nick kicks me in the lower back, and I stumble and skid across the dusty floor.

The door slams shut.

The heavy latch bangs closed.

16

"Let me out of here, Nick! God damn it!" I clamber to my feet and slam into the door, but the shock wave reverberates through my body and pulsates in my sore shoulder.

My eyes take a minute to adjust to the dark. Sparse light filters in through a small vent on the side wall, but otherwise, the garage is black. I lean against the door and try to gather my bearings. Nick's footsteps shuffle the rocks outside; he's walking toward the front of the building. I shouldn't have trusted him. He's talking, but his voice is too muffled to understand him, so I tiptoe across the grimy floor and put my ear against the big garage door.

"... I didn't ... No, I just put him in there ... Well, shit. How was I supposed to know, man? ... He ain't getting out of there. Not with that bar across the door ... Yeah, I'll stay ... All right."

I am screwed. Up the creek without a paddle or a boat and cinder blocks tied to my feet. I tug on the garage door, but it only lifts about an inch off the ground thanks to the giant padlock that I just now remember. Damn. I step back and bump into the SUV. How the hell did Lindsay's car end up in here?

My eyes have adjusted to the darkness, so I peek in the rear windows. Nothing. I make my way to the passenger-side window. The inside of the car is empty. I walk around the hood to the driver's side.

Oh no.

Lindsay lies on the ground, her hands and feet bound behind her back.

I kneel beside her. "Lindsay? Lindsay?" My hands quake. "Lindsay?"

I'm petrified. I fear she's dead. I'm scared to touch her, to make that a reality.

I blow out a breath and reach down to touch her skin.

She's warm. Hot, even.

It's too dark to see her face clearly. There's a tool chest to my right, so I slide a drawer open and feel around, hoping to hell there's nothing sharp in there. Screwdrivers and wrenches. I open another drawer. I reach in, and my thumb strikes the switch of a flashlight. I grab it and shine it near Lindsay.

There's a deep purple lump on the side of her forehead and a line of crusty blood oozing from a cut above her eyebrow.

My stomach turns. What the hell happened? I untie the nylon rope bound to her wrists and ankles, careful not to move her head.

"Lindsay? Can you hear me?"

She moans, her eyes flutter behind their lids.

"Hey. It's Chad."

Lindsay's eyelids part, one before the other. Her eyes are scrambled, unfocused.

"Don't move, okay?" I reposition myself so she can see me without moving her head. Despite my clamminess, I grab her hand and squeeze.

She gives a weak squeeze in return. "Chad?"

"Hey. I'm here. Are you okay?"

"What…what happened?"

"Uh, it looks like you got hit pretty good on your head."

She reaches for the wound and winces upon touching it. "Where are we?"

"I think we're in Wade Linford's garage." I want to ask what the hell she was doing. Did she come here snooping around? What was she thinking? My heart rate is skyrocketing.

"Oh."

I suck in a deep breath and let it out slowly. "Do you know what happened to you?"

"I…I came to break into the big building. There—" She clamps her eyes shut and grimaces. "Ouch." She huffs. "There are windows on the other side. They're…they're blacked out. I couldn't see in, so I broke one. I started to climb in. But a guy was in there."

"Wade?"

"No. A skinny guy. Buggy eyes."

A dizzy spell strikes out of nowhere and almost knocks me over. I brace myself and shake it off. The fever is threatening to erupt, but I fight with every cell in my body to prevent it.

"There weren't any cars here. I didn't know anyone was here." She stifles a sob and stiffens her face. "Chad?"

"Yeah?"

"Thank you for coming after me." Her lips tremor.

I didn't know you were here, I say in my head. "Of course," I say out loud.

Lindsay pushes herself up into a seated position and leans against the driver-side door of her SUV. "My head feels like a tornado."

"Try not to move. You have a pretty nasty bump on your forehead. Did the skinny bug-eyed guy hit you?"

"I…maybe? He came after me. He had a…like a pipe or

something. I can't…can't remember."

"Okay. We'll get out of here. Do you have your keys or phone?"

She clumsily pats her pants pockets. "No." Her voice is faint.

"Anything in your car that might help us?"

"I don't…I don't know. I'm so tired." Lindsay's head slumps down onto my shoulder.

"Lindsay?"

She goes limp. Soft snorts escape with each breath she takes.

I click on the flashlight and scan my surroundings. A red padded creeper seat used for rolling underneath a car. The tool chest. A workbench littered with magazines, crushed beer cans, and an unopened package of shop cloths. I can use that. I gently scoot to my left and ease Lindsay's head to the hard ground, then grab the shop cloths and tear open the packaging. I tuck the pile of cloths under Lindsay to give her a relatively comfortable pillow.

Now to find a way out of here. I spin in a slow circle, the flashlight's weak beam a yellowish spotlight on the innards of the garage. On the wall next to the walk-in door is a switch. I step around Lindsay and flick it. A panel of white tube lights illuminates. The center of the garage is lit, but the corners remain dark. I wonder if Nick can see the light on from outside. I don't think it matters, but the thought stays with me.

My best option is to get Nick talking. And I have to do it before Wade or anyone else gets here. I lose grip on the flashlight but catch it before it falls to the ground. Damn sweaty hands. Touching and infecting Nick would be a bonus.

I press my ear to the roll-up garage door. I don't hear Nick. I'm certain I would have heard his Jeep if he left, though, so he's still out there. Probably.

"Nick?" I yell through the door. I peek at Lindsay, but she doesn't stir. "Come on, man. It doesn't have to happen like this."

Nothing.

And then...gravel shuffling. Getting louder. A stray rock clangs against the metal garage door.

"Listen. Get us out of here, and I'll help you with the money. I mean it."

Silence.

"Nick?"

"Man, I can make three or four grand a week working for Wade. You seem like a decent dude, but ..."

"Then let us out because it's the right thing to do. You're not a killer."

"I told you...nah, man. If I let you out, Wade's going to cut me off again. Or maybe worse."

"You can let us out, then tell Wade we overpowered you and escaped."

Nick laughs. "Yeah, that'll make me look good." His footsteps scuff the rocks. "Sorry, man."

Damn it. What are my options now? Defense? Nick has a gun, and Wade is going to be armed. I look around. The wrenches and screwdrivers could be used as weapons, but they won't do much against a gun. I open the tailgate of Lindsay's SUV. Spare tire. Tire iron. Mini jack. Jumper cables. Not much to work with. I look inside the glove box, the center console, and under the seats. Nothing but papers, a brush, lip gloss, and two stale fries.

At least we won't starve to death.

I gently close the passenger door and walk around to the other side of the SUV toward the tool chest. Inside the first drawer, I find a Leatherman multi-tool, a Swiss-army-knife gadget that has pliers, a saw, a blade, and various other tools. This could be handy. I set it on the workbench and continue my search through the tools. My fingertip finds the business end of a pick, so I slide the pointy tool out and set it next to the multi-tool. I open another drawer and discover a long, sturdy torque wrench used to remove wheel lug nuts. My arsenal is complete.

"Chad?" Lindsay says.

I jolt back, my reflexes set on high tension. I bump into the workbench, and the multi-tool clangs on the ground between the workbench and the tool chest. Fantastic.

I turn to Lindsay. "Hey," I say, catching my breath.

"What's going on? Did I pass out?"

"Yeah. Just rest right now. I'm going to get us out of here."

"Wade is going to kill us, Chad." Her eyes are steely; she no longer looks lost inside her own head.

"Well, not if we can get out of here. It's just Nick outside."

She wrinkles her brows.

Outside, the gravel crunches under a heavy vehicle.

Two doors slam shut.

Lindsay's eyes and mouth grow wide in unison.

My throat plummets into my chest.

We both look at the roll-up door as if it's going to speak to us.

Nick says, "Hey, Wade. What's up, Dwight? They're in there."

17

I press my ear against the roll-up door.

"You left the man untied?" It sounds like Wade.

"Yeah," Nick says. "But he ain't getting out."

"I know he isn't getting out. It's what he might do when we try to go in, dumbass."

"Oh. Sorry, Wade."

"Dwight, take this idiot with you and get them bound. I bet he untied the woman, so they're probably both free now."

"Got it." Dwight speaks like he has a sock stuffed in his mouth. "Get your gun out, Nick."

The lock outside scrapes against the metal. Three bangs on the roll-up door ring out through the garage.

"You will have three guns aimed at you when this door opens," Wade says. "Don't try any funny shit, got it?"

I back away and stand in front of Lindsay. I whisper, "Act like you're passed out."

"Okay." She lies down and closes her eyes.

"Got it?" Wade says, agitated.

"Yeah, got it," I say.

The door rolls up, and blinding sunlight gushes in. I squeeze my eyelids tight. When I open them, I see Wade in the entryway on the right, aiming a handgun at me. Nick is on the left side, gun raised. Between them stands a lanky man holding a pistol at his waist. The skin on his face is tight like it's pulled back and tied behind his head. His enormous eyes are yellowed and bulging. He looks like a chihuahua deciding whether to shake or piss itself.

I put my hands in front of me, sweaty palms up.

Wade steps in. "I don't know what the fuck you two were planning here, but I hope you've made your peace with God." He looks at Dwight and gestures toward me. "Use duct tape this time."

Dwight stashes his gun in his waistband and lurches past me toward the tool chest. Three of his four front teeth are missing, and the lone tooth looks like it's hanging on by a thread. Tools clang and clunk as he sifts through the drawers. "Got it." He looks down at Lindsay, then up at me. "You first."

Maybe I can touch him quickly and infect him. I might not live through the day, but at least I won't have to suffer. I put my hands behind my back.

"Makin' it easy. Smart." He pulls out a length of tape, and the rubber-stretching sound sends chills through me. He shuffles close and grabs my right wrist. He yanks my arm back, and fiery pain rifles through my shoulder. I scream in agony. Dwight grabs my other wrist and wraps tape around them both. I wiggle my fingers, stretching toward him to make skin-to-skin contact. I grab for his wrist, but he avoids my touch. My hands are bound painfully tight. The adhesive tears my arms hairs out with any movement. I wiggle my fingers, trying to make contact with his skin, but he steps away, and I am stuck with the virus's raging symptoms.

"Check his pockets," Wade says.

Dwight stands in front of me and pats me down. "He's got nothin'."

Wade looks at the tools I set on the workbench. "Put those tools away and lock the chest."

Dwight follows the command. He turns to Lindsay. "Now it's Sleeping Beauty's turn." He crouches and tapes her wrists. I'm surprised how delicate he is with her, considering he bashed her head and gave her a nasty concussion earlier today.

Lindsay deserves an award for her acting skills, pretending to be passed out.

I hope she's still pretending.

Wade steps close to me and jams the barrel of his gun into my ribs. His face is inches from mine, so close I notice the pores on his nose filled with blackheads.

"You work for Gutierrez?" He sneers as he says the name.

I shake my head. I've never heard of anyone with that name.

"Right." He draws the word out. "Then what the hell are you doing here?"

Lindsay grunts and works herself into a seated position. "You killed my cousin."

"Oh, looky here. This one's alive." Wade smirks. "Who the hell is your cousin? Never mind, I don't care." He steps away from me. "Take care of them, Dwight."

"All right. Here?"

"No, stupid. I don't want blood all over my shop. Take them to the spot."

"Do we have any tarps?"

Wade looks down his nose at Dwight. "Can you just do it without the tarp?"

"Well, it's just easier to keep everything clean. Remember that Mexican guy?"

Wade groans. "Fine. Go check the office."

"K." Dwight scampers out of the garage toward the small

rectangular building.

"You're a fucking asshole," Lindsay says, seething.

"I know, honey."

"Wait," I say. "Just take me. Let her go."

He laughs, a deep cackle that sounds like a wounded animal. "Nick, keep guard on the garage. I have to get today's load ready." Wade walks out of the garage and reaches up to the door. He locks eyes with me. A grin slowly forms on his bearded face. He winks, then lowers the door until it slams to the ground. A metallic clunk rings out as the lock closes.

A prickly chill trickles down my spine.

I will not see tomorrow.

Worse than that, neither will Lindsay.

I don't know what Dwight plans for us and his tarp, but it isn't something I look forward to. Lindsay hasn't said a word since Wade and his boys left us here. I guess I haven't, either. It's tough to think of something to say when your death is moments away.

I lean against Lindsay's SUV and slide down to sit next to her. "How's your head?"

She rolls her eyes and shakes her head. "Hurts. But I'm so pissed off I don't really notice it." She breathes through her nose. "I want to rip Wade's smug face off and force-feed it to him."

That's...graphic.

I close my eyes and lean my head back onto the door with a thump. The duct tape is impossible to wriggle out of. I've resigned myself to dying. I'll give Dwight a fight—I won't make it easy on him—but I know ultimately there's no way out of this alive. I accept it as fact.

"What's that?" Lindsay asks.

I open my eyes and direct my eyes to her focus under the workbench.

The multi-tool! A surge of electricity streams through my veins. I lie on my side and scooch like a half-paralyzed worm to the workbench. I spin on my butt and try to fit my leg underneath so I can kick the multi-tool forward, but my leg gets stuck just above the knee. I spin again and face Lindsay.

"Can you stick your leg under there and kick it out?"

"I'll try."

She moves in the same awkward fashion. Watching her awkward jerks and jolts makes me smile, despite the situation. Lindsay gets to the bench and makes quick work of the task. She kicks the tool out from underneath, and it scrapes across the floor, coming to a rest near the rear tire of the Subaru.

"That's perfect." I wiggle my way back to the car and scoop up the multi-tool. It takes some maneuvering to open it and expose the saw blade, but after a few patient minutes and two bloody fingers, I cut the duct tape away from my wrists. The process is slow, but I'm finding success.

"Is it working?" Lindsay asks.

"Yeah. I'll get yours cut off in just a minute."

Hopefully, before Dwight returns with his tarp.

I free my hands and start immediately on Lindsay's. I cut through her tape in less than a minute.

She stands and wobbles a bit. "Now what?"

I rub the raw skin of my wrists that were involuntarily Brazilian-waxed. "Now we come up with a plan. I don't know how, but—"

"I'm not going down without a fight." She tightens her lips, and a fire rages in her eyes.

"Right on. Help me look around for anything we can use, like a weapon or a distraction."

Lindsay looks at the roll-up door's tracks, then to the walk-in door in the back. "We should jam the garage door, so they have to come in the back."

I smile. "That's brilliant." I move too quickly, and my balance sways. If I die, it won't be before I infect Dwight. I steady myself and search the garage.

Lindsay is in the corner by the walk-in door. "What about this?" She holds up a crowbar.

"Nice. Let's try it."

She brings it over and wedges it behind a wheel on the track. The metal clangs.

I shush her.

"Sorry." She grimaces. After a few tries at different angles, she says, "I don't think it's going to work."

I inspect the track. "There's a hole just above the wheel. If we can get something skinnier, it might work."

"Hang on." Lindsay goes back into the corner and returns with two spools of galvanized aircraft cable—thin wires twisted into a sturdy metal rope.

"That's perfect."

"Here," she says. "You take this one and tie up this side, and I'll do the other."

We each loop the aircraft cable through the holes in the tracks and around the wheels. Three minutes later, the garage door is inoperable.

"Okay, so now they'll come in through the back," I say. "What are we going to do when that happens?"

Lindsay cocks an eyebrow. "Bum rush whoever comes in?"

"Maybe. But they'll have at least one gun. Let's keep searching the place. There has to be more stuff we can get creative with."

Lindsay disappears into her corner in search of more valuable treasure. I scan the shelves lined with grease-stained boxes. I find a bundle of yellow twine, a Phillips-head screwdriver with electrical tape around its handle, and a funnel.

"Any luck?" I say.

"Sort of." Lindsay walks over to me carrying a roll of fishing line, an awl, and a rubber mallet.

I show off my trove. "All right, what can we do with this stuff?"

"Maybe a tripwire with the fishing line?" Lindsay says. "Then smash him in the head with the mallet." She touches the wound on her head and scrapes some dry blood off with a fingernail.

I pick up one of the shop cloths she was lying on earlier and hand it to her. Our hands brush, and the giddy tingles of a thirteen-year-old shoot up my spine.

"Thanks," she says. "Hey …"

"Yeah?"

"How did you know I was here, anyway?"

A lump catches in my throat. I don't know why I feel guilty, but I do. "I, uh…I didn't." My voice embarrassingly raises two octaves.

"Oh." Lindsay drops her focus to the floor. "Why did you come here then?"

"The same as you—to find something incriminating to take to the police. Fucking Nick…he tricked me. Said Wade screwed him over, so he'd take me here and help me find something." Boiling anger floods, heating my neck and face more than the fever has. "But he's using me to get back on Wade's good side."

Lindsay grabs my hand. "I'm glad you're here."

Her skin is cool against my clammy palm.

"Look, I know why you want me to go to the doctor."

She looks up at me, concern etched in lines on her forehead.

"You're right," I say. "If we make it out of this, I will go to your doctor. I promise."

She smiles. Then hits me playfully. "Maybe if you would have decided that sooner, we wouldn't be in this mess."

We hug. I've missed this comfort. No more taking it for granted, I promise myself.

Over her shoulder, I notice a shelf with various fluid containers. "I want to continue this hug, but..."

"Yeah. Let's get out of here, first."

I go to the shelf and pull down a bottle of transmission fluid. "Can you—"

A heavy vehicle crunches over rocks as it nears the garage.

A door slams.

Footsteps.

A metallic clank, then the roll-up door rattles. "What the hell?" Dwight says. "Ah, damn it. It's jammed again."

Shit.

"Lindsay," I walk her to the rear passenger side of her SUV, "lie down here and play dead."

Her eyes grow wide, and her mouth drops open, but she says, "Okay," and lies down.

I pour the red transmission fluid on the floor around her head. The puddle covers a five-foot diameter. I slide the bottle under her car and jog around to the random collection of supplies I gathered. I grab the taped-handle screwdriver and the crowbar.

The metal rod clangs outside the rear of the garage.

I run on the tips of my toes and sidle up next to the door.

The rod scrapes against the door.

I reach across and flick the light switch off.

The door handle turns.

18

The door scrapes the dusty concrete as it swings open.

I look at Lindsay. In the dark, the transmission fluid looks even more gruesome than I'd hoped.

I don't know if I'm ready. I've never attacked someone like this.

The door opens fully, sunlight spilling in.

"What the ..."

Now's the time. My hands shake.

Dwight lurches in, gun drawn. I slam the crowbar onto his wrist, he yelps, and the gun clatters on the floor.

I jab the screwdriver into his neck.

Jab. Jab. Again and again, his hot blood spurting on my arms.

He looks at me, eyes shot wide, his mouth locked in a silent scream. He falls to the ground like a pile of dirty laundry.

I grasp him by the wrists—his skin slimy from the gore—and drag him to the dark corner of the garage. He stares up at me, his face still long with shock. I have to look away.

I don't feel better yet, the virus's grip is still tight, so I wipe my hand on my shirt and pull up his pant leg, then grip his ankle. Dwight groans. My fever evaporates. The itch disappears. The Grim Fever symptoms fade, but my stomach turns, and acid boils in the back of my throat.

I've never killed anyone like this before. Dwight's face, frozen in a scream, will haunt me along with all the victims I've infected with the virus.

I shake it away for now and pick up his gun.

"Chad?" Lindsay whispers.

"Hey." My voice is shaky and unrecognizable. I sound like an imposter.

"Should I stay here?"

"No, get up. I don't know if Nick or Wade heard him—"

Footsteps running on the gravel outside.

Shit.

"Stay there," I shout-whisper. I tuck myself behind the door.

"Dwight, what's going on?" It's Nick. His footfalls hit the concrete just outside the door.

"Hey man, what—oh, shit. Dwight?" Nick walks in but stops on the other side of the door. I sense his presence but cannot see him.

"Dwight? What happened, man?"

Lindsay moans.

Nick's shoes scuff the dusty floor.

"Shit. Chad? Where's Dwight?"

I have to act while I still have surprise on my side. I lean everything I have into the door. It slams into Nick, bounces off of him, and swings open again.

He grunts and spills backward. He catches himself on Lindsay's SUV, but he's prone, the gun to his side.

I raise my gun, flip on the light, and step toward him.

His face twists with confusion.

"Drop it," I say in the most savage voice I can muster.

He doesn't move.

"I will shoot you in the face."

"Chad ..."

I step closer. "Drop the fucking gun."

It thunks on the ground.

"Kick it this way."

He does.

Lindsay stirs and stands up.

Nick's eyes flick to her. Then to Dwight's body behind me. "Oh, fuck. Chad...what did you do to Dwight?"

"That same thing I'm going to do to you if you don't shut your goddamn mouth. Lindsay? I need your help."

She comes to my side.

"There's some twine on the workbench."

"Got it."

Lindsay snatches the bundle of yellow twine and stands behind Nick. "On your knees," she tells him in the most commanding voice I've ever heard.

Nick follows the order.

Lindsay binds his wrists and wraps the thin rope around his body at least a dozen times, pinning his arms to his body. Has she done this before? She must've seen it in a movie. I hope. She rejoins me with a smirk painted on her face.

"Where are my phone, wallet, and keys?"

Nick blinks twice. "I gave them to Wade."

"Where's Wade?"

"He's in the big shed. Chad, let me go, man. I can get you out of here, I swear. Please, I have a new baby, and—"

"Shut the fuck up. Stand."

Nick sighs, leans against the vehicle to get his feet underneath him, and stands upright.

"Wait," Lindsay says. She walks around the other side of her car, then returns with a shop cloth and a strip of duct tape that once bound one of us. She jams the cloth into Nick's mouth and roughly applies the tape. "There."

I give her a quick nod and a smile. Behind her, the open door invites freedom. Pine trees sway as the wind tickles their needles. Birds tweet at each other. We'll be out of here soon. I can taste it.

Only one more hurdle.

I slide the bar into the lock, trapping Nick inside the garage.

"What about the thing you used to cut our tape?" Lindsay asks.

"Shit. I didn't think of that. Well, we don't have time to worry about him."

I peek around the corner, unsure if Wade heard the commotion. A bird caws and flies overhead. It lands on the roof of the barn-like building.

Lindsay presses against me and peers around the garage. "He's in there, right?"

"That's what Nick said."

"It's two on one." She holds up Nick's gun.

The last thing I want is a shootout with a militant. "Is there another door to that place on the backside?"

"No, just the door that faces the trailer. There's nothing on the backside except blacked-out windows. One of them is broken."

"Okay." I peek around the corner again. Still clear, so I brace myself against the wall and slink toward the front of the garage. No Wade. My truck sits in the same place I parked it. Nick's Jeep is in the same spot. Another truck is backed up near the roll-up door, and a large blue tarp lines its bed. The engine is running.

This is it; we're free!

I squeeze Lindsay's arm. "Come on, let's get in and get the hell out of here. We can call the police from a gas station or something."

She pulls away from me. "No. This will not end with him going to jail." The look on her face says she's not leaving here until Wade is dead.

"What happened to getting evidence to take to the police?"

"Fuck that. That was before that scrawny bastard knocked me out. Before Wade told that goon to kill us."

"Lindsay—"

"Don't 'Lindsay' me. That asshole killed Frank. He killed that kid a few years ago. Who knows how many people he's murdered and killed with his drugs. Chad, he wants to kill us. You think he's going to just shrug this off? No." Her upper lip curls into a snarl. "Wade Linford deserves to die."

"I know he does. But getting out of here alive is more important. That truck is running. We can leave right now."

"No." Her shoulders writhe as she seethes. She pushes past me.

I grab her wrist. "Wait. Listen. If you kill him, you'll only feel good about it for a minute. Then he'll never leave you. His ghost will stick in your mind forever. Believe me, I still see the faces of everyone I've killed. It's not worth it."

Lindsay's jaw tightens. Her eyes sharpen into a narrow focus. "I'm not leaving until he's dead."

I shake my head. "Fine. Then at least let me kill him. You don't need to carry that burden."

She shuts her eyes. "Fine."

"All right." I blow out a long breath, half-relieved and half-surprised that Lindsay relented. I point to the front of the building. "Let's wait for him to come out of there. He probably has his gun on him, but if we catch him by surprise, we should be able to take him out without turning it into the OK Corral."

We tiptoe across the gravel to the backside of the large shed. I whisper, "I'll go around the other side."

Lindsay nods once and slinks along the wall toward the front of the building, stepping slowly over the gravel. She holds the gun to her side.

A sudden realization strikes. I don't know if she's ever shot a gun before.

I suck in a deep breath and peek around the back corner. It's clear. The gravel gives way to grass, thankfully. I walk along the outside of the building with deliberate steps. I reach the first of four tall paneled windows and take a quick glance inside. Nothing is visible through the black plastic that covers the inside of the window. I duck and pass under it, unsure if it's more translucent from the other side. I do the same for the next two windows. The third window is busted out in the lower-left quadrant; its plastic covering whips in the breeze. I crouch and listen for any movement inside. It's quiet save for the rustling of the makeshift curtain.

I walk on my knees underneath the window. I look up to the camera perched on the corner of the building. I remember seeing two on the other side. Hopefully, no one is watching the feed at the moment.

I step forward to stand upright.

A gunshot rings out.

I recoil.

Lindsay screams.

"Hello, girlie," Wade says.

19

I raise my gun, terrified of what I'm about to see, and jump around the corner.

There's nothing in the front of the building, but I hear heavy footsteps in the gravel leading to the parking area.

Lindsay.

My heart thumps like a machine gun.

I peek around the corner of the building. Wade squeezes Lindsay's waist with one arm and clutches a gun in his other hand. He carries her like a squirmy toddler toward the garage. She kicks her feet wildly but hits nothing.

"Cha-ad." Wade taunts like a schoolyard bully. "I've got your little girly friend, here." He stops in front of Nick's Jeep, facing the roll-up door. "Come on out."

He thinks I'm in the garage.

He's too far for me to take a shot without risking Lindsay. And I can't make it to him across the gravel without him hearing.

Lindsay wriggles a hand free and punches Wade on the shoulder and chest, but it doesn't faze him.

"Oh yeah, I like 'em feisty."

I step away from the edge of the building to gather my thoughts. My foot hits something solid.

Lindsay's gun. She must have fired and missed, and either she dropped it, or Wade knocked it away from her. I pick it up and stuff it in my back waistband.

I peek around the corner again.

Wade stands with his back to me and positions Lindsay in front of him, the barrel of his gun pressed against her head. "Open up!"

The garage door slides open.

Wade pulls the gun away from Lindsay and fires before the roll-up door is all the way up.

Nick falls to his knees, a crimson splotch blossoming on his shirt. He falls face-first to the ground.

"What the fuck?" Wade yells. "Where's Chad? Fuck! Dwight?"

He throws Lindsay to the ground.

My truck is ten yards away.

"You lied to me, you little cunt."

I sprint across the gravel toward it.

He points the gun at her head.

"No!" I yell as loud as I can.

Wade whips his head around, followed by his firearm.

Pop! Pop! Pop!

A bullet whizzes past my ear.

One shatters my truck windshield.

I don't know where the third one went.

I dive behind my truck, the engine block between me and Wade.

"Wade, wait. It's me you want. Let her go."

Gravel shifts.

"Stay still, sweetie," Wade says.

Lindsay lets out a panicked grunt.

"Let her go."

"You think I'm stupid?"

"We can all just walk away from this." I'm out of breath.

"No. We can't." He huffs. "Not all of us, anyway. I'm going to kill you. Then I'm going to have some fun with this one. She's ballsy. I like a good challenge."

Shit.

We overplayed our hand.

I should have made Lindsay get in the other truck. We'd be far from here and safe.

I peek through the window. Wade stands over Lindsay with a boot pressed down on her neck and his gun aimed at my truck. I can't get in a position to take a shot at him without exposing myself.

She's struggling, punching his shin and kicking at him.

I have to keep him talking.

"Wade. How did you survive Grim Fever?" I don't know where the thought comes from. It's a desperate move.

He snaps his head in my direction. "What? How did —"

"Because I infected you."

"You?"

"Yeah. After your protest at the post office."

"The sweaty hand guy? That was you?"

"Yeah."

I have no plan other than to keep him talking. If he's talking, he's not killing. Or doing worse.

"No shit. Small world, eh, Chad?"

"Listen. I know you get the symptoms. They suck, right?"

He laughs. "Yeah. Feels like six hangovers all at the same time."

"Lindsay has it, too. There's a treatment. It feels like bad allergies, that's it. No fever. No terrible rash. No sweaty palms."

Wade looks down at her. "That right? Your boyfriend gave you the Grim, too?"

"Fuck...you." The words sputter as she struggles to get them out.

Wade presses harder on her neck.

Her face goes red. She swings her fists at his leg but lacks the strength for any meaningful impact.

"Wade, let her up, and I'll tell you the combination of medications."

"Oh yeah? We're gonna make a little trade? I let your girlfriend go, and you tell me to take two ibuprofens and some green tea?" He laughs, a deep throaty cackle that makes me cringe.

"What will it take then? For you to let her go?"

"I'm not really in the mood to negotiate. I have a delivery I need to make, and my guy is missing. Would you know anything about that, Chad?"

Shit. I'm losing this.

"I'll do Dwight's job. I'll be your bitch. Anything, just let Lindsay go."

"You're funny, Chad. Dwight's replaceable. Nick's replaceable, too. He's actually more valuable to me dead, the fucking idiot. You're nothing to me, Chad. You're a cockroach on my garage floor. But Lindsay here...I can make some money on her. You know how much a pretty young thing like this goes for?"

This sick fuck...

"I can get a few grand if she's already doped up and mellowed out. How does that sound, Chad? Ship her down to Venezuela or over to Russia? Find herself a nice man." He lets out a gruff laugh. "More like fifty men."

He's antagonizing me. I can't react; that's what he wants.

Lindsay's face has turned purple, and a vein on her forehead is bulging. Her eyes are only half-open.

"Of course," Wade says, "I'd have to give her a run myself. You know, to make sure the product meets a certain standard."

Don't react.

"She's cute. Maybe I'll keep her for myself."

I want to gouge his eyes out. I want to tear his tongue off and stuff it down his throat, let him choke on it.

Don't react.

Think. What does he want?

"I have money." I shout the lie, hoping he takes pause. "I have over a million from an inheritance."

"I have money, too. It's not about money." He chuckles. "Well, it's not all about money. I'm wiping away the scum of the earth. The reservation. Mexico. The blacks. Hell, even the trashy whites who suck on the government's tits. So, yeah. I don't care about your money."

He lowers his gun.

My hand flinches, adrenaline gushes. Is this my chance to get a shot off?

Wade bends over and grabs Lindsay by the neck. He pulls her up.

I'm not confident I can't get a shot off without hitting her.

She's limp.

No.

Her head lolls to the side.

"Ah, shit," Wade says. "Looks like I broke your girlfriend." He slams her to the ground.

She drops like a rag doll, limp and lifeless.

React.

I stand up and fire at Wade.

He ducks behind the blue Jeep.

I try counting my shots, but I lose track. I stop firing and duck behind my truck.

I peek over the hood. Lindsay lies on the ground. Her face ashy, her lips pale, a line of blood dripping from her mouth.

"You done now?" Wade says.

I try to shake away the image of Lindsay's lifeless face, but I can't. I choke back the tsunami of emotion about to break through.

"You fired a lot of rounds, Chad," Wade shouts. "You got any left?"

I couldn't save her.

"Look, bud, I've got things to do."

I failed Lindsay.

"Can you just stand up and let me shoot you so I can get on with my day?"

Wade has to suffer.

"Sorry about your girlfriend. I really hoped I could enjoy her."

Sick fuck.

"You know, this isn't my first Mexican standoff. I've got things to do, but I'm a patient man."

As long as he thinks I have ammo left, he won't risk getting shot.

I get up as quietly as I can.

He's still behind the Jeep.

I tiptoe backward toward the big shed, ready to fire if he pops up.

"I might still have a go at her. She's still warm. Wouldn't be the first time."

Wade's voice grows quieter as I slip farther away.

I make it to the corner of the shed, then turn and sprint around the backside. My legs feel sturdy, pumping with purpose.

Lindsay's face. I can't escape her listless face.

I have to focus.

I get to the opposite side of the shed and peek around the corner. I see Wade's foot, but Dwight's truck blocks my view.

He's still talking.

I might be able to make a run for the truck. It's still running. I might have a decent chance at escape, but Wade would have an open chance at shooting me.

And I don't want to leave Lindsay here. Not like that.

Another idea forms.

I creep from the building to the truck.

I peer underneath the chassis. Wade crouches behind the driver-side front tire. I can't see his head, which direction he's facing.

I consider making a dash for the garage, but I'm standing in gravel, so he's going to hear me. If I tiptoe, I'll be exposed. I need to know which way he's looking, so I lean past the taillight, hoping to hell his focus isn't aimed this way.

Wade is looking through the driver-side window.

"I'm getting bored, Chad."

I make my break for the garage, steady and quiet. Each step feels like a lifetime. The gravel shifts under my shoe, but I manage to make it to the garage wall unnoticed. I lift the locking bar, mindful not to make any noise.

The garage smells like rotting death. I glance at Dwight in the corner. Flies have already taken place in their buffet line. I step around the puddle of transmission fluid and lean against the wall beside the half-open roll-up door. Uncoiled aircraft cable lies on the floor, a bundle of yellow twine lies next to the multi-tool.

I kneel and take a quick peek outside.

Wade is still looking through the window, his back to me.

He holds his gun with both hands, arms propped up on his leg.

"Look, there's gonna be four other guys showing up here in about half an hour. They'll see you when they pull in."

I have a clear shot.

"Time is on my side, buddy."

I slide a knee to the right.

Steady the gun and take aim.

He shifts the gun to his left hand and pushes himself closer to the front of the Jeep.

Exhale.

I squeeze the trigger.

Wade's hands explode in a red cloud.

He screams.

I duck under the door and run to him.

He spins onto his ass and leans against the tire.

"You fucking ..." He raises his arm, the soupy lump of mangled flesh oozing blood. "My hand!"

I stand over him and aim at his chest.

"Does it hurt?" I ask.

"Feels great." He smirks with endless defiance, then lowers his disfigured limb.

I step onto his bloody stump and put all my weight on it.

Wade yowls involuntarily, then straightens his face. "You're a sick fuck." He sneers.

I point the barrel of the gun at his chest.

"What are you waiting for, pussy?"

I pull the trigger.

Click.

I'm out of bullets.

Searing pain stabs through my calf.

I fall to the ground, the butt of a knife handle sticking out of my leg. He moved so quickly I didn't even notice that he had a knife.

Wade scrambles for his gun, leaning on the elbow above his destroyed hand.

"Dumbass."

He clutches it.

I reach behind me and draw Lindsay's gun.

I fire.

Wade falls to the ground. A red hole above his left eye fills with blood, his wide eyes and gaping mouth permanently etched on his face.

I crawl to Lindsay, grab her cold body, and pull it onto my lap.

Tears flood down my face.

"I'm so, so sorry." The words are nothing more than a creaky whisper.

I couldn't save her.

I failed her.

She hated Wade so much she wanted to kill him.

And he ended up killing her.

I hold Lindsay tight and weep as if my tears will bring her back to life.

Every negative emotion imaginable shakes me to my foundation. Guilt rises above me like a dark cloud. I know it will never leave me.

20

"I know you blame yourself," Ron says. Lindsay's brother-in-law sets a water bottle on the kitchen table in front of me. "But Lindsay is…gone because of Wade Linford. Not you."

"Thanks." I unscrew the cap and take a long pull. I wipe my mouth and set the bottle on the table.

Ron and Kristin's house is full of Lindsay's friends and family. The kitchen counter teems with finger foods and soda cans, and the scents of deli meats and cheese blend with the odor of cheap wine. People I don't know stand around and chit-chat. A loud male voice in the living room announces that a company called Creston Widmer has developed a Grim Fever vaccine, and it's in the final trial. Lindsay's sister, Kristin, sobs in the hallway while her children run around giggling.

Ron's eyes are red, but he carries his composure like a professional. He looks like a stoic secret service agent in his black suit and tie. "I know it's no consolation—we all would rather have Lindsay here—but that guy wasn't just a drug dealer. He's into all kinds of evil. You shut down one of the worst criminals in the state of Washington." He smiles weakly and pats me on the shoulder.

Waves of emotion either crash into me with no warning or suck me out into an ocean void of feeling. In this moment, I am numb.

Monica walks into the kitchen. She hugs Ron. "Kristin needs you."

Ron nods and leaves.

"Hey, Chad," Monica says.

I force a pathetic smile.

"Can I get you a plate of something? We have a ton of food."

I shake my head. "No. Thank you."

She grabs my hand and squeezes. "Okay."

A minute after she leaves, I get up and make my way through the hall toward the restroom. I pass Kristin, who is now crumpled on the floor weeping with Ron on his knees, consoling her. It kills me to see her in such pain.

I close the bathroom door and examine myself in the mirror. Dark circles surround my eyes. My skin is ashy, cheeks sunken in from lack of appetite. I splash water on my face and open the door, unsure of where to go. The hall is teeming with people trying hard to not have a good time. Most of the funerals I've attended give off a strange energy where people think, "It's great to see so-and-so, but I can't act too excited."

I sift through the crowd and look into the backyard. No one is out there, and that's the company I'd prefer to keep at the moment, so I squeeze through cousins and aunts and high school friends and find myself alone on the patio.

I made a promise to Lindsay, and since her burial was only an hour ago, now feels like as good a time as any to fulfill it. I pull my phone out of my pocket and call the number for Lindsay's doctor to make an appointment for Tuesday. After the call, I clutch the phone at my side and close my eyes. My ghosts visit. First comes Leanne, my beautiful wife. She's smiling, but her face blurs into the dozens of prisoners I infected and sentenced to death. Now Wade's sneer infects my mind. I wish I could kill him again. And again. Dwight's face, locked in a scream, sends a cold burst down my neck. Finally, Lindsay's face appears with her sweet, muted smile and those eyes that send my blood rushing.

My phone buzzes and jolts me out of my visions. I look at the screen.

Unknown number.

My first instinct is to throw the damn thing onto the ground, but I stare at the screen instead, wondering if this is the person that has been calling me the past few weeks.

I tap the green icon. "Hello?"

"Oh, my gosh. You answered," an excited woman's voice blares through the speaker.

"Who are you looking for?"

"Chad Chaucer. That's you?"

"Yes. Who is this?"

"Oh, hi. My name is Ada Curry. I work at Creston Widmer Pharmaceuticals."

"Okay. And why are you calling me?"

"I can't believe I tracked you down!" She sounds like a giddy high schooler.

"What's this about?"

"Sorry. Um, I tend to ramble. Uh, so you were infected with the SVE-1 virus two years ago, and I think you might be in serious danger."

PART III

21

"What do you mean I'm in danger?"

"There's a government agent," Ada says. "She's gone rogue, and she's trying to track you down."

Dr. Choi?

"How do you know that?"

"Well, she was working with my company to trace people infected with SVE-1 virus, but...she turned against us. She's off doing her own thing now. And we don't trust her."

I consider telling Ada that I've already encountered Choi and her now-deceased partner, but I'll keep that to myself. A man in a navy blue suit comes outside and pulls out a cigarette. He turns his back to me as he lights it. I move to the side yard and find the shade of a pine tree.

"And you think she's coming after me?"

"Mm-hmm."

"Why?"

"My guess is she wants to take you in. The numbers of people infected..." She lets the words hang.

What does Ada know about me? Does she know about

Lindsay? About Wade? Are there any other survivors?

"Why would she take me in?"

"For all the…incidents at the various prisons you've worked at."

Shit. Ada knows about the prisons. That must be how she traced me.

"I'm sorry," Ada says. "I don't mean to be so blunt."

"It's fine. So, you assume this agent is coming to arrest me. Why are you telling me this?"

"We want to find a cure for SVE-1. And I suspect your blood—since you're one of the few known survivors—can give us the answers we're looking for."

"So, you take a blood sample. And then what, I get arrested? Go to jail for those incidents you mentioned?"

"Mr. Chaucer. Chad. I can't promise what will happen to you after we get your sample, but at least you can have knowledge that you're helping to find a cure."

I look inside through the window. Lindsay's family and friends mill about in black dresses and suits, mourning the loss of an incredible woman. A woman I infected, who should be alive today. Yes, Wade Linford killed her, but she wouldn't have gone after him if I hadn't found him and passed the virus to him.

"Chad? You still there?"

"Yeah. I'm here."

"Well, what do you think?"

"No idea." Something is off. This Ada person knows so much about me and my past. Am I thinking too much? Is it possible to help without walking into a trap? "How can I get a blood sample to you?"

"We'll buy you a plane ticket to Pittsburgh, and you can come to our lab."

A cold blade slices through my chest. I haven't been back

home since the weeks following Leanne's death. I vowed to never go back.

"Pittsburgh?"

"Yep. It's the only way to guarantee a fresh sample."

"I thought you had a vaccine in the final testing stages."

Ada snickers. "There's a vaccine in the final testing stages, but it won't work."

"Why not?"

"Don't get me wrong, it might help a few people have less severe symptoms. Maybe save some lives. But it's not a cure. We need you for the true cure."

"This all seems a little weird. Why would you hire a government agency to trace survivors? That doesn't seem normal. Where did the virus even come from?"

Ada sighs, the puff of air deafening through the phone speaker. "Look, Chad. I could be in serious trouble for saying this, but I want to be honest with you, so you feel comfortable trusting me."

She goes quiet.

"Go on," I say.

"Well, SVE-1 isn't a naturally occurring virus. We created it to—"

"You made the damn thing?"

"Y-yes. The virus out is a prototype for a universal viral vaccine."

Warmth floods my neck and rises into my ears. My free hand balls into a fist. "You're telling me your company created the worst virus in the history of humankind and let it out?"

"Not intentionally, Chad—Mr. Chaucer."

"Oh, so you made the deadliest disease in the world by accident. Got it."

Ada sucks in a breath. "I'm aware how bad it sounds. But I promise you, we were on the path to curing all viral infections.

Everything from cold sores to AIDS. The goal was a single virus to destroy all other viruses. We designed our virus to be contagious, so we could minimize the number of dosages required to treat everyone across the planet."

"Well, guess what? It doesn't work."

"No, not yet. But it will. And your blood could help us get there sooner."

"How did it get out? Did you deliberately infect some poor schmuck?"

"No. Never! It was a total accident. My lab assistant touched a contaminated surface and became infected. No one knew about it at first. He infected three people outside of the lab — that we are aware of. You were one of those people."

"Lucky me."

"I'm so sorry. We traced the other two people, and they died within five days. My assistant, too."

"And why did you bring in the federal agent? To cover it up?"

"No." She says the word like it stole the last of her oxygen. "We wanted to make sure it didn't spread." She sniffles. "We didn't know there was another infection until after your wife died. We couldn't find you on our own, so we brought in Agent Choi to help."

Choi.

"And why did she turn against you? Why am I in danger?"

"I told you because she wants to apprehend you."

Choi had the chance to detain me and didn't.

"I still don't see it. Why haven't they taken me in by now?"

"I—I don't want to scare you," Ada says in a near whisper, "but she killed someone. Our CEO had a private security officer accompany her. And now he's dead. The security guy, not the CEO."

I wonder if she's talking about McNulty. "So why does that

mean I'm in danger?"

"I mean...she's dangerous. Who knows what she intends to do to you? Your best hope is that she just wants to arrest you and bring you in alive."

"You didn't answer my first question. Why did she turn on your company? None of this makes any sense. Why didn't your company speak to her supervisor or someone else at...what agency did you say it was?"

"I don't know, Mr. Chaucer," she replies in an angry whisper. "I'm just a biochemist. They make those decisions way above my head. My boss just wanted me to contact you to get a blood draw. I've already told you way more than I should have. I get it, this all sounds crazy, but can you help? Help us come up with a vaccine to save lives."

I should hang up. This company created a virus, let it out, then let loose a crazed Fed to clean it up. Why should I trust them? Yeah, giving my blood to save lives sounds noble, but I don't owe this company anything. In fact, my wife is dead, Lindsay is dead, and tens of thousands of others are dead because they unintentionally let a deadly virus out of their building.

No, I'm not helping them. They've ruined my life. Two years of a living hell. They don't deserve my time or my blood. Hell, I should tip off the Pittsburgh news stations and expose what Creston Widmer has done.

"Chad? Mr. Chaucer?"

I pull the phone away from my ear.

"Hello?" Ada's voice comes out faint with the speaker at a distance. "Chad?"

I tap the red icon to end the call.

22

I stare at the black phone screen. Did that just happen? The lingering numbness from watching Lindsay's casket descend into the ground bleeds into anger from the call with this Ada Curry person. I grow more furious as I realize Ada is one of the people responsible for my life being torn apart. My thoughts twist into a whirlwind of emotions that I am not equipped to handle right now.

I return to the patio. The smoker left, but the stale odor of burned tobacco still lingers. The late afternoon sun casts long shadows on the ground like gray ropes squeezing the world. I plop into a cushioned chair and rub my face. Someone slides the glass door open, but I don't look up.

"Oh, Chad," Kristin says. "Sorry, I didn't think anyone was out here."

I lift my gaze to Lindsay's sister. Her eyelids are red, raw from the constant rubbing. She forces a sad smile.

"Hey, Kristin. I was just about to leave." I stand.

"Oh. You don't have to go." She fumbles with her hands and sits across from me. "Please, stay." She crosses her left leg over the other and tugs at the lace near the bottom of her black dress.

I have no words for her. My mind is in a million places, nowhere near here.

"Too many people in there," she says. "I needed a breather."

"It's a good turnout," I say like it's a garage sale rather than a funeral. "Seems like Lindsay has a ton of people that care about her."

I wonder how many people would show up to my funeral. Less than a dozen. I keep the thought to myself.

"Yeah. Lindsay...she was a remarkable person."

"I'm so sorry I couldn't do more when—" I cut myself off. I can't finish that statement out loud. What do I say to Kristin? When Wade Linford crushed her neck with his heavy boot? When he picked her up by the throat and dropped her like a ratty doll?

"No." Her voice shakes. "You shouldn't apologize for anything." She sucks in a deep breath. "You know, when she was in the hospital with the infection..." She coughs. "Sorry. I was so scared of losing her. She used to sneak into my bed at night when we were little, terrified of sleeping alone. I was her protector. When she was in the SVE-1 unit, we couldn't even see her. The thought of my baby sister dying alone shook me to the core. I just thought, 'Poor thing; she has to go through this all by herself.'"

Kristin stares off into the void.

"But she made it," she says. "She's always been tough and strong-willed. When she got out of the hospital, I squeezed her so tight, she joked I broke her ribs." Kristin chuckles and wipes away a tear. "I never wanted to let her go."

"I wish I could have known her longer," I say. What I keep to myself are the constant arguments she and I had.

"She loved you, Chad. I know you guys had your

disagreements, but she loved you."

Dagger in the heart.

"I loved her, too." The words catch in my throat as my face grows damp under my tears. "I promised her...I promised I'd make an appointment with her doctor. To get the treatment."

Kristin shuts her eyes tight. "Lindsay would be happy about that." She stands and walks over to me. She grabs my hands, and when I stand up, she pulls me into a hug. Sobs shake both of us, and I'm unsure who it's coming from. Kristin squeezes hard.

"I think you might break my ribs, too," I say.

"Sorry. I guess I'm a strong hugger." She pulls away and laughs. "Thank you, Chad. You weren't together long, but thank you for making her happy while you were."

I nod but don't dare speak for fear of another dam-breaking flood of emotion.

"I'm glad you made that appointment. There's something special about you and Lindsay. Maybe the doctors can help find a cure by examining you." Kristin draws in a breath. "Okay, I guess I should get back inside." She smiles at me before she slides the door open and disappears into the crowd of mourners.

Kristin's words idle in my mind. I should want to help, to buy back some karma. Right my wrongs and all that. But something inside me holds me back. Distrust of that Ada woman is part of it. And some part of me wants to keep suffering. Even if that means others will suffer.

I wasn't always such a selfish asshole.

The smoker in the navy blue suit comes outside again. He raises his brow at me, then pulls out another cancer stick. He flicks his lighter and ignites the tobacco. The odor reminds me of casinos and dank bars, two places I've thrown away plenty of money in my darker times. I hate that smell, so I get up to go inside, but two young women I don't recognize come through the door leaning on one another, cackling, and uttering drunken exchanges. They stand in the doorway, beer bottles in-hand, unaware of anyone around them.

"Excuse me," I say.

They ignore me.

"Can I get through, please?"

"Oh, sorry!" One giggles and the other breaks into full-on belly laughs before they part enough for me to fit through.

It feels like thirty more people have shown up since I went out back. I can't move without touching everyone around me; never have I been more glad to not have the Grim Fever symptoms active. I squeeze my way through the crowd. The noise has shifted from consoling chatter to boisterous partying. I spot Ron in the kitchen. He waves me down, so I fight through the congregation toward him.

"Hey, can you help me close this thing down? It's getting a little rowdy, and Kristin wants it to be over."

I want to leave, drive until I run out of gas, swim in my head for the rest of the night. But it's the least I can do for Ron.

"Sure. What do you want me to do?"

"Tell people that the party is moving to Lonely Lou's Pub. It's down the street on Sharp, right by the campus."

"You got it."

I wind my way through the various clusters of people, telling them about the bar, that Kristin and Ron thank them for coming, that it's time to head out. Most people oblige, while others continue their conversations as if I were invisible and silent. I peek outside. The twin drunks still block the door. Terrific. I slide it open and poke my head outside.

"Hey ladies, the party's moving to Lonely Lou's. You know where it's at?"

They look at each other and laugh.

I sigh. "Everyone's heading there now. Better go if you want a good spot."

The one on the right eyes me. "Are you coming?"

What response will convince them to leave? I shrug.

"We'll save you a seat," the one on the left says. They giggle some more. I step aside and gesture. They walk in and head to the front door.

The blue-suit smoker grins. "You want a wingman, bro?"

"No, thanks."

He stubs his cigarette and the ground and shrugs. "All right, man." He goes inside.

I pick up a few cups and bottles left on the patio tables. I bring them inside and toss them in the trash can.

"Thanks, Chad," Ron says. He shuts his bedroom door. "Kristin's in bed, but she said to tell you goodnight."

"Please give her my best."

"I will. And please, don't be a stranger. If you ever want to talk, have dinner, or grab a beer...we'll always be here."

"I appreciate that, Ron." I can't imagine hanging out with Kristin and Ron without Lindsay. They're good people, but that would be too awkward.

He comes over and reaches his hand out. I flinch and jerk my hand back—old habits and all that. Quickly, I smile and shake his hand.

"Hey, I realize it won't change how you're going through right now, but in the eyes of the department, you're a hero for taking out Wade Linford."

I muster a 'thank you' even though I don't feel like a hero. No, I'm a selfish villain who's killed people just so he can maintain his lonely existence.

I nod to Ron and walk out front toward the street where a few cars remain parked. Three people stand at the tailgate of a pickup, making plans for the rest of their evening. Beyond them, a couple is making out next to the red sedan parked behind me. I get in my truck and start the engine. I don't want to go home. And no way in hell do I want to go to Lonely Lou's with the funeral crowd. So, I shift into gear and head to the place that's been circling in my mind.

On the drive, my thoughts flitter between Lindsay, the woman from the pharmaceutical company who knows all about me, and Grim Fever. I shouldn't have symptoms again for another two or three weeks. When I do, I have an inmate in mind. And thinking of Ada, I wonder what resources she has to track me down or if Choi's the one who did the legwork.

My phone rings and drags me from my thought tunnel. Unknown number. Of course. My first instinct is to ignore it, but my thumb disagrees with me and taps the green icon.

"I told you, I'm not going to Pittsburgh."

"Sorry! I'm just calling to ask if you're still in contact with Lindsay Green. She's not answering my calls."

Nothing about this is funny, but I let a small laugh escape. I pull into the parking lot of the Starbucks, where I first met Lindsay. "I just left her funeral."

"Uh," Ada says, though it sounds more like a choked gurgle than a word. "I'm…sorry. I wasn't aware she passed."

"Murdered." I don't mask my anger-ridden grief. "By a drug dealer. Who was also a Grim Fever survivor."

"What? Oh, my gosh. How…"

"How what?"

"How are there three survivors?"

"You're the scientist; you tell me."

Ada doesn't respond. She clacks on a keyboard, humming an unrecognizable tune. I'm about to hang up, but she clears her throat. "You infected Lindsay…"

I can't tell if it's a statement or a question.

"Yes." I don't know why I'm wasting my time with this.

"Did you infect the other person? The drug dealer?"

"Yes."

"Interesting." More typing. More humming.

It takes all I have to maintain composure. I want to scream into the phone. Instead, I inhale and say, "Look, I wish I could help you, but I'm hanging up now."

"Wait, please. Have you infected anyone else? After those two?"

"No." Technically, I infected Wade's henchman, Dwight, but he was already bleeding out, so I don't think it's necessary to include him.

"Okay. Oh my gosh, this might be the breakthrough we need." Her words ooze with giddiness. "Is there any chance I can convince you to come to my lab? The virus is mutating, and I need to compare my baseline with the virus in your system."

I'd be lying if I said I wasn't curious about finding the reason Wade, Lindsay, and I survived. But going to Pittsburgh? Where my life with Leanne started and ended? I don't know if I can bring myself back there.

"Chad? You still there?"

"I'm here."

"I know it's a lot to ask, but—"

"No."

I end the call and blow out a heavy breath. I can't go back there. Too many memories, too many ghosts.

A white-haired man in a navy jacket walks through the empty parking lot toward the Starbucks entrance. He's wearing yellow rubber gloves—the kind used for cleaning rather than the medical-type gloves most people wear in public these days. I remember when I first came to this Starbucks, looking for someone to infect. No one knew at the time to wear gloves.

I thought coming here might help me. With what, I don't know. But going inside doesn't feel right.

I put my truck into gear and aim for the exit.

23

The examination table paper crinkles with every movement. I tilt to one side and try to straighten it, but there's no use. I've never understood the point of this stuff. It either bunches or sticks to you, exposing the padded table anyway. A quick double-knock on the door catches my attention. A half-second later, a woman in a full hazmat suit enters.

"Mr. Chaucer," she says, her voice muffled by the plastic screen of her PPE. "I'm Doctor Reed."

"Hello."

"So, you have SVE-1 symptoms?"

"Yes."

She writes with a stylus pen on a tablet computer. "Are you experiencing any symptoms right now?"

How much info do I give her to treat me without her discovering I've been carrying this curse for two years? "No, I'm not."

"Can you describe your symptoms?"

"Yeah. Uh, sweaty palms, painful rash, and fever. Sometimes my body aches."

"Huh." She scribbles something on the tablet. "It says here you first noticed the symptoms two weeks ago?" She looks at me with pinched eyebrows.

"That's correct." That's a lie.

She glares into my eyes, expressionless. She nods once, then writes on her tablet. "Have you made skin-to-skin contact with anyone in that time?"

"No. I wear gloves any time I'm in public."

"Good." Her eyes move to my baby blue gloves. "Do you know how you became infected?"

"I think from my girlfriend." I feel a chunk of flesh gouged out of the pit of my stomach with every lie.

"Did she receive treatment?"

"Yes. She recommended you."

Doctor Reed looks at me for a few seconds, then makes a note. "I'm required to mention that we will log your information in a national database. It's not a big deal; it's just something we're required to do for all SVE-1 patients."

I swallow hard. "Okay."

"Why'd you wait so long to come in?" she asks, the clinical tone of her voice gone and replaced by angry disappointment.

"I don't know. The itching and stuff wasn't bad, so I didn't think it was as serious."

"It's very serious, Mr. Chaucer. This is the most contagious virus ever. You may have infected other people."

If only she knew.

"I'll write you a prescription. You need to avoid going out in public if you have sweaty hands, a fever, or if a rash develops."

"Okay."

"The nurse will go over the medications." She leaves without another word.

Guilt bubbles in my gut.

Five minutes later, a nurse comes in with my medicine in a bag. She only wears a facemask and surgical gloves. "Use the cream for your hands and anywhere you have a rash. Results should be immediate, and it will help prevent contaminating any surfaces you touch. You should still always wear gloves." She sets the bag next to me and takes two steps back. "Take the pill at the first sign of symptoms. It should help with the fever."

"Okay. Thank you."

"Questions?"

"I don't need to take a test?"

"We're not testing for it anymore. We just assume anyone who thinks they have it has it."

"Oh."

"Any more questions?"

"No. Thank you."

"Okay." She leaves, and it seems like I've disappointed the doctor and the nurse. But I know it would make Lindsay happy that I went through with it.

The officer's locker room at the prison is steamy and smells of soap and sweat dueling for odor supremacy. I put my duffel bag on the bench and sit. Footsteps approach from my right, and I cringe. Dalton—who was Nick's best friend—uses the locker next to me. He has done nothing but stare daggers at me since his buddy's death. He blames me for Nick's death despite the police report explaining in detail how Wade killed him. Never mind that Nick would've left me for dead. Facts don't seem to matter to Dalton.

"Your bag's in my way," he grumbles.

I swallow the words threatening to escape my lips and place it on the other side of me. I take off my shoes, change my socks, stand up, and take off my shirt.

"Whoa, Chaucer, what happened to you?" It's Miller, one of the few I like.

"What do you mean?"

"That bruise on your back. Looks nasty, man. How'd you get that?"

I haven't fallen. No bruises I'm aware of. I peek over my shoulder but can't see anything.

"Here." Miller hands me his shaving mirror.

Between my shoulder blade and spine, I see the start of a deep purple rash, about three inches in diameter.

No. It's too soon for this. I should have two weeks at the very least.

Shit.

I sense Dalton's eyes burning holes into my flesh. "Oh," I say, faking a laugh. "I was moving some boxes in my closet and backed into a shelf. Didn't realize it left a bruise." I hand Miller the mirror.

"Where are you starting today?" he asks.

"Yard. You?"

"Cafeteria. What about you, Dalton?"

Dalton makes a sighing grunt sound. "Yard."

Fantastic.

I finish dressing and slide my hands into a pair of baby blue gloves, then report to yard duty.

"Enjoy the fresh air, boys," Miller says as I follow Dalton out.

Dalton circles the perimeter of the yard. Every time I glance at him, he's scowling at me the same way he scowls at the inmates. A fiery itch pulsates under my shirt. It's spreading, inching its way across my back, and my hands are sopping wet inside the rubber gloves. Not ideal, but at least I can test out the medicine. This unrelenting itch is driving me insane, so I need to take care of it, or I'll explode.

I make my way to Dalton, cool and casual...I think. "Hey, Dalton, can you cover for two minutes? I had a bad burrito, and it's working its way through me."

Dalton's eyelids lower half-way. "Seriously?"

"Sorry, man. I'll make it up to you."

He shrugs. "Whatever. Just don't take all day."

"Thanks." I head back to my locker, glad I left the medicine in my duffel bag. The locker room is empty. I dry-swallow the pill and spread the cream on my back. The nurse said there would be instant relief, but it still itches. I apply more ointment to my back and hands. The itchiness is as bad as ever.

"Damn it."

Time for Plan B. I've already pegged my next target: a toothless serial rapist named Jared McConnell who has been stomping around like he owns the place. I like to have a plan in place before I set out to infect an inmate, to time it right after a visit with family or their lawyer, but time is short, and a deserving prick is in my sights.

Back into the yard, I nod at Dalton. He glares at me and turns away. The scorching rash climbs up my neck. I rub my skin against my collar, but it's useless. I have to act now.

Jared McConnell sits at a picnic bench playing checkers surrounded by four of his cohorts. A black swastika tattoo on the back of his shaved head stands out in any crowd. He's brash, always demanding to be center stage. It's only a matter of time before he'll need some extra attention.

"Eat shit, pussy," he yells at his opponent. "King me!"

The man across from him, Jones, flips the board. "Man, fuck you."

McConnell slams his palms on the table and bolts upright. "You wanna go, bitch?"

I might not be waiting too long.

Jones stands up. A mob swells, and a staticky voice over the radio calls for backup in the yard.

It's go time.

I run to the table, sliding up the glove on my right hand to expose my clammy palm, eager to grab Jared McConnell's tattooed arm. Bodies pile in, the inmates jockeying for position to witness the fight. Out of nowhere, Dalton slams Jones on the back with his baton. Jones falls to the ground, and McConnell jumps in and starts kicking him. Dalton yanks inmates off the pile and tosses them left and right, landing blows with his baton on whoever comes near him.

I shoulder my way through the crowd. Two steps away from McConnell. I reach for him, but someone pushes me from behind. I crash to the ground. To my right, Dalton is beating Jones while McConnell is standing over him, kicking Jones in rhythm with Dalton's baton. Someone kicks me in the ribs. A fist or a foot finds the back of my head, a throbbing knot forming immediately. I get to my knees, trying to stand against the wave of the testosterone-fueled crowd. An inmate smashes into me, sending me flailing onto my back. Another inmate lands on top of me, pinning me to the ground.

Fists meet flesh, batons meet bone. Screams, groans, curses. Scuffling. Shouts from officers and prisoners. I can't breathe with the weight of this man on my chest. A body collapses next to me. Jones, bloodied and battered, lies motionless on the ground, inches from my face. I can't see McConnell. Something smashes into my temple, and my vision flashes white for a second. Everything is a blur now. A hollow ringing in my ear muffles the noises of the brawl.

The man isn't crushing my chest anymore. I don't know how or when he got up. I can breathe. A hand grabs mine and pulls me up.

"You okay, Chaucer?" It's Miller.

I shake my head, trying to regain composure. I stretch my eyelids wide, but my vision is still off. "Got kicked." My voice comes out muffled. Am I slurring?

"I know, come on." Miller guides me into the hallway. My head feels like the inside of a church bell, and my legs wobble under my weight. We make it to the infirmary, and they lay me on a bed. It feels like the padded table in the doctor's office but without crinkly paper.

"Dude, you got swallowed up by the mod," Miller says. "And what the hell got into Dalton?"

"I don't know." I try to recall what happened, but every thought is a medicine ball smashing into the inside of my skull.

A nurse comes in and tends to me. I only catch half the things she says. Everything looks like I'm on the teacup ride at Disneyland. Miller leaves at some point.

I close my eyes. The nurse is talking, tells me to sit up. I do as she commands and put my hands in my lap. They were sweaty earlier today, but they're fine now. I remember I had a rash, but I'm not itchy. My head hurts. Was I wearing gloves? Yes, I put them on after I put on the—

Oh shit. Where are my gloves? Who did I touch? The nurse? Miller?

Panic sears through me like a fiery arrow. I infected someone, and I have no idea who. I can only hope it was an inmate. Or Dalton, because fuck that guy. If it was Miller or the nurse, I'll never forgive myself.

24

Yesterday's incident at the prison has my head spinning. I suppose getting kicked is the primary reason for that, but I'm lost and need to ground myself. This morning, I woke up and got in my truck for an aimless drive to clear my head, trying to remember the first person I touched with my exposed hands. The poor bastard I infected. It's bad enough knowing you've sentenced someone to death, even the worst of human trash, but not knowing? This is a new breed of guilt.

I've driven for two hours, and now I find myself at Starbucks again. Lindsay's Starbucks. I slide out of my truck, and an emotional weight draws me to the ground. Memories and thoughts collide, and part of me wants to get back in and drive until the tank is empty. Instead, I stride to the door. To my right, the white-haired man in yellow gloves from the other day shuffles towards the entrance.

I hold the door for him.

"Thank you," he says. He stops and looks me in the eye. "You remind me of my grandson, Daniel."

I remember this guy; he was here the day I met Lindsay. He

told me then that I looked like his grandson. "Well, you're too young to be my grandfather," I say.

He grins and walks inside.

"What are you drinking today, sir?" I ask him.

"Oh, I just get the regular hot coffee. Those fancy drinks are too sweet for me." He stares off into the void, and his face turns downward. "My wife loved the Frappuccinos, though. Caramel was her favorite, but she always got the peppermint one during the holiday season."

"Can I buy your drink?" I ask.

He snaps back into the present. "Oh, no. You don't have to —
"

I feel an overwhelming urge for kindness. I attribute it to Lindsay's influence on me. "Please. I insist."

"Well, if you insist."

I order our drinks, and we sit. He takes the chair Lindsay sat in the first time I saw her. The seat beside him is open, so I sit.

"I'm Clarence, by the way," he says. "I'd shake your hand, but…"

"Oh, I understand. Chad. Nice to meet you, Clarence."

The blenders whir, and the milk steamer whooshes. The scents of roasted coffee beans and various sweeteners fill the air.

"What do you do for work, Chad?" Clarence asks.

"I'm a correctional officer at the prison."

"Oh, that's quite a job, I imagine."

"It's never dull."

Clarence smiles.

"What about you?" I ask. "What did you do to pay the bills?"

"I taught math at the university. Forty-one years. Retired for a little over twenty. Hard to believe."

"It's incredible you stayed there for so long."

"It's where I met my wife, Doris. We both worked there, both enjoyed it, so we saw no reason to leave." His face goes long again, his eyes lost in memory.

"Order for Chad," the barista calls out.

I get up and gather our drinks. Clarence smiles when I hand him his. "Thank you." He removes the lid and blows on the hot coffee.

"Doris and I came here four or five times a week. We loved seeing the different people coming and going. People watching, she called it."

I remember Clarence's wife; Lindsay gave up her chair, so Doris could sit.

Clarence blows on his coffee and sips. "We used to make up stories about the people we'd watch. 'Oh, that's Suzy Jane with her husband, William. They're getting coffee before they rob the bank next door.'" He smiles, but his eyes are sad.

"Doris sounds like a fun lady."

"Yes, she was. She really was." He draws in a long breath and lets it out. "She died a week ago. Alone in the hospital. I couldn't even be with her." A single tear glides down his cheek to his chin. He wipes it away. "Nothing worse than dying alone."

A hollowness forms inside my chest, and guilt swirls in my stomach.

"That Grim Fever." His tender voice turns dark, angry. "That's why I couldn't be with her."

I don't know if I should leave or console this man I just met. Lindsay would console him. So would Leanne. I'm not as good as either of them; I didn't deserve either of them.

"We joked about living to be a hundred," Clarence says, his light and tender voice back. "When she first passed, I thought there was no way I'd want to live that long alone." He sips. "But she would want me to. She wouldn't want me to give up just because she's gone." He looks me in the eye. "During our last conversation, she said, 'We only get one life, so you'd better live it making the people who love you proud.' And she's right. She's gone, but I can still make her proud."

A warmth floods over me. It takes all I have to hold back a volcano of emotion. "Those are wise words," I say with a creaky voice.

Clarence nods. "Doris was a wise woman."

We sit in silence, sipping our hot drinks. Clarence looks around. The only other customers are two teenage girls staring at their phones.

Clarence nods toward the girls. "Those two," he says under his breath. "They're waiting for a message from the CIA. Their mission."

I smile. "One of the baristas is a Ukrainian spy. But which one?"

Clarence looks at the employees behind the counter. "Oh, it's the blond in the glasses. No doubt about it."

A bored twenty-something leans on his elbows, blond hair flopping over one lens of his tortoise-shell glasses.

I nod. "It's definitely him."

Clarence laughs, an unexpected booming laugh that doesn't fit his appearance. I laugh, too, to the point of watery eyes. After gathering myself, I check the time. "Ah, I need to get going. It was great meeting you, Clarence."

"Likewise. Thanks for the coffee and the company."

"You're very welcome. I'm sorry to hear about Doris."

He nods. "I'll keep coming here and playing the people watching the game. It would make her proud."

"I'm sure it would. Okay, take care of yourself."

"I will."

I nod and stroll toward the exit. I pull out my phone and call Ada. It's time to make Lindsay and Leanne proud.

25

The deboarding process goes fast since the flight was less than half full. It's terrible that the airline industry hasn't recovered from the lockdowns of the Grim Fever outbreak, but I won't complain about having an entire row to myself.

I ponder the impact of the virus when it strikes me that, despite all the damage I've caused, my blood will not only help create a vaccine but will also help to revitalize the entire economy. I frown. It's a nice thought, but not one I have any business taking credit for.

I order a Lyft from my phone and scan the airport. Stores and restaurants in the terminal are closed, an odd sight for a Monday afternoon. Pittsburgh isn't the biggest city by any stretch, but it's not a sleepy flyover town, and seeing the airport this empty creates a hollowness in my gut. It makes me miss the usual sights of people slaloming through crowds to catch their flight or travelers huddled in front of a monitor searching for their departure gate. Normal times when, with the typical hustle and bustle of any airport, germs spread from person to person at an alarming rate. I'm cautious when the symptoms flare, but how many people passed the virus without knowing?

I stand in the middle of the baggage claim. Only one belt is moving, about a dozen people around it waiting for their luggage. Guilt slithers into my thoughts, knowing that I had a huge part in the spread of this miserable virus.

My phone buzzes and pulls me out of my darkness. My ride is approaching, so I step outside.

The Lyft driver stops at the curb—Ken in a white Prius. He rolls down the window. "Chad?"

"That's me."

Ken gets out and pops the trunk. "Oh, no bags?"

"Nope. Just here for the day."

I get in the backseat while Ken plops into the driver's seat. The clear plastic barrier between the front and back gives me the impression of the back of a cop car.

Ken looks at me in the rearview mirror. "So, you're heading to Creston Widmer Pharmaceuticals, huh? Business meeting?"

"Yep." I don't feel like giving the full explanation.

"Where you coming in from?"

Most days, I wouldn't mind a chatty driver, but I'm in no mood to have a full conversation with a stranger. "Spokane."

"Ah, nice. My brother-in-law's from Seattle."

I don't pay any attention to Ken's one-sided conversation. The plastic divider muffles his words anyway. I pull out my phone as we enter the Fort Pitt Tunnel and scroll through old photos. Selfies of Leanne and me, pictures she took of me goofing off while playing mini-golf, shots of her doing cartwheels in the grass by the river.

I can't believe I'm back in our city. I miss her, and I've never been more alone. This is more difficult than I imagined. I clear my throat to fight back the emotion building in my throat.

"Ah, damn it," Ken says.

Yellow flashing lights bounce off the tunnel walls.

"They've got a lane closed up ahead. Sorry."

"No problem." I'm supposed to meet Ada in thirty minutes. I send a message telling her I'll be late and close my eyes.

An hour later, we come out of the tunnel, and my heart does a double-pump. The tall downtown buildings stand stark against the steel-gray sky. I didn't think I'd miss this city, but I'm home.

Ken eases through traffic. We drive past the soccer fields Leanne and I played at. The bars and restaurants we frequented with our friends. The park where we'd lie in the grass and imagine one day chasing children. So many memories turned to ghosts.

We pass the turnoff that would take us to my old neighborhood. I'm half-tempted to ask Ken to take a detour, but I want to meet with Ada and get this over with. Being in Pittsburgh now gives me the same bubble-gut I had as a kid, ditching school and begging to get into trouble. A minute later, we pull onto a small side-street and stop in front of a gray building that has the architectural flair of a shoebox.

"I guess this is it," Ken says.

"Thanks. Have a good one."

"You too."

I pull out my phone and give Ken five stars and a twenty percent tip, then walk into the double glass doors. The lobby is drab, nothing more than a desk and two fake potted trees. Not what I'd expect from a pharmaceutical company. I don't know what I should have expected, but this isn't it. A security guard sits at the desk, looking at his phone. With his thin mustache and pimples, I'd guess he's less than two years out of high school.

"Excuse me? I'm here to see Ada Curry."

The guard looks up and pulls out his earbuds. "Hey. How

can I help you?"

"I'm here to see Ada Curry."

He pushes a button on his desk phone. "Someone's here for Ada. She'll be out in a minute," he says without looking up. He pops his earbuds back in, and his attention retreats to his phone screen.

I don't bother thanking him.

I find a corner to stand in since there are no chairs. Two minutes pass before a door opens behind the charming security guard. A woman with wavy brown hair streaked with strands of gray comes out. "Chad? I'm Ada." She smiles and waves me toward her. "Thank you so much for doing this!"

Her appearance does not match her young and bubbly voice. I expected an excitable cheerleader type, but Ada is older than she sounds, maybe in her early fifties. She has a warm smile and big brown eyes. More soccer mom than cheerleader. I guess today's theme is misplaced expectations.

"Sorry I'm late," I say. "Traffic in the tunnel."

"No problem! Let's go." I follow Ada into a hallway. She carries a small brown leather bag with both hands. "I'm so excited to get working on your blood! This is going to be great. How was your flight?"

"Pretty empty."

"Yeah, not too many people traveling these days."

We pass dozens of doors. No windows, no signs.

"The building is a bit more modest than I expected."

"Oh, yeah." She laughs. "We've only been in business about two years. Peter Creston, he's our CEO, started the company after working at another big pharma place that I will not name." She looks over her shoulder at me and smirks. "He came up with an arthritis medication and wanted to sell it on his own means rather than watch the big company take all the credit. So, he got a loan from his mother-in-law and started this. If we get the SVE-1 vaccine nailed down, I'm sure we'll move into a nicer facility." She smiles again.

We reach the end of the hall, and Ada pushes open a door. We descend a flight of stairs, then go through another door and into a parking garage.

"Where are we going?"

"Well, with your concerns about the…legal stuff, I thought we'd do this off the books, so to speak. We'll go to my house, draw your blood, and that's it."

"Okay." This is weird. But I'd rather not go to prison, so I go along with it. "I appreciate you considering that."

"Of course!" She slows her pace. "And, not to scare you, but I'm not sure if Agent Choi is having the lab watched. So, I thought we'd be extra safe."

If that's supposed to make me feel better, she failed.

Ada picks up her pace again. I search the garage, trying to guess which car is hers. There are around three dozen cars. Ada keeps walking straight, passing all the SUVs and minivans. Perhaps she drives a luxury car. Or a sports car. Tesla. She's going to surprise me with a Tesla. Instead, we come to a staircase, and Ada walks up. I follow her, and at the top, we find another door. She opens it, and we're on a small side street.

"We're not driving?" I say.

"Nope. My place is right over there." She points across a small park, where a quaint cluster of townhouses lies.

I follow Ada across the street and onto a walking path laid out in the grass.

"You're sure you won't get in any trouble for doing this?" I ask.

"No, I don't think so. If I can get two vials of blood back to my lab, everything will be fine. And don't worry, I'll sterilize everything." She smiles.

"Okay."

Her phone rings. She looks at the screen and tuts. "Hello? … Yes, I'm working on it … I know, I'll get it done as soon as I can … No, you don't need to … Okay. Got it."

Ada puts her phone away. "Sorry, the lab supervisor keeps pestering me about a report." She points to a brick home sandwiched between a blue unit and a yellow unit. "This is it," Ada says. The hinges squeal as she opens the door. "Home sweet home."

I follow her inside.

26

I'm seated at Ada's kitchen table while she preps for my withdrawal. A French door opens to a small backyard on my left, and a paneled window to my right exposes the room to a flood of sunshine. There are dark red curtains on the door and window, chicken and cow knick-knacks here and there, an old metal jug in the corner. The space is modest, but it's homey.

"Just about ready." Ada pulls on light blue medical gloves.

Her phone rings. She looks at the screen and tuts. "Ugh, leave me alone," she says to herself as she ties a small band a few inches above my elbow. She presses on my vein and swabs my arm with an alcohol wipe.

Her phone rings again.

Ada sighs. "Sorry about that," she says. She tries to sound calm, but now she's agitated.

"No worries," I say, though I'm not sure I want her anywhere near my exposed skin with a needle now.

She moves the needle toward my arm. "Okay, you're going to feel—"

Someone bangs on the front door.

"Ah, damn it!" Ada sets the needle on the table and unwraps the tourniquet. "I'll be right back." Gone is her warm smile and cheery demeanor. She gets up and leaves the kitchen through the front hallway. This day can't get any stranger.

A faint shuffling near the back door steals my attention. I turn to find Choi standing inside the doorway, her gun raised, and a finger to her lips. My heart rate triples. I flinch, but there's no way for me to get up and around the corner before she shoots. So I sit back and raise my hands.

"What the hell?" Ada says from the front room.

Choi steps closer and stops five feet away from me. She glances at the items on the table. Ada's bag, the syringe, wipes, and vials. She raises a finger and cocks her head back at a slight angle.

Ada's footsteps grow louder. "There was no one th—" She comes around the corner, and when she sees Choi, she bolts back toward the front door.

Choi doesn't move, her face set like an iron statue.

The front door bangs against the wall.

"What the hell?" Ada screams. "Let me go!"

Who the hell else is here?

Choi grips her gun with both hands and aims it toward the kitchen entrance off of the hallway.

Something thuds against the other side of the wall, followed by other unidentifiable commotion. "Get your hands off—" Ada says before her voice shifts to muffled grunts.

Seconds later, a massive man comes into the kitchen. He's wearing a gray suit, and his hair is shaved close enough to display fat rolls on his scalp. He's got a grip on Ada, his meaty hands enveloping her shoulders. At some point during the struggle, he handcuffed her and stuffed something in her mouth to keep her quiet. She wiggles free and tries to run, but he grabs her and brings her in tight.

"Thank you, Miguel," Choi says. "Take her in."

Miguel nods once and takes Ada away. I'm not sure if I'm more scared for her or myself.

Choi stares at me, her gun now lowered to her side.

I was wrong; today is far more bizarre than I could have ever imagined.

27

Choi holsters her gun behind her back. I might get out the back door before her draw, but I don't know if there's another Miguel outside. Besides, I have nowhere to run. I can only hope that Choi isn't interested in anything that results in my death.

Choi stares into my eyes, her face showing no emotion. "Hello again, Mr. Chaucer."

"Are you here to arrest me?"

Choi's eyebrows pinch together. She shakes her head. "No."

"What agency are you with? FBI?"

She presses her lips together in a tight line. "I'm here for Ada Curry."

"Ada? Why? What the hell is this?"

"Do you remember, Mr. Chaucer, when we first met? I told you there was more going on than you realized."

"You gave me a concussion last time I saw you, so my memory is a little shaky." The words fall out before I can filter myself. Sarcasm will not help me in this situation.

A coy smile forms on Choi's face. "Allow me to go back.

Had you heard of Creston Widmer Pharmaceuticals before Ms. Curry contacted you?"

"No, I don't think so."

"Most people haven't. In the interest of time, I'll summarize. Peter Creston, the company's founder and CEO, hired my firm to help with contact tracing when the SVE-1 virus was first released. I discovered some inconsistencies and realized I needed to investigate Mr. Creston and his company."

"Wait, your firm? Are you a lawyer?"

"No." She draws in a deep breath through her nostrils. "I specialize in...fixing things."

So she's not government. Interesting.

"So," I say, "contact tracing is tracking down infected people, right? You were trying to find the people infected by the guy—Ada's coworker who was accidentally infected?"

"We'll revisit that point, but yes, that's the general idea."

"So that's why you were tracking Lindsay down in Spokane?"

"Yes. But when I learned that you, too, were infected, I found the trail that leads you back here."

"And what about that McNulty guy? Ada said you killed him and turned on them."

"Your police officer friend killed him."

"And you almost killed the officer." Heat bubbles beneath my skin at the thought of Ron lying there bloodied and near death.

"If I wanted someone dead, I wouldn't shoot them in the shoulder." Her coy smile returns. "This is all hypothetical, of course."

I don't know what to believe or who to trust. I rub the stubble on my face.

"What were the inconsistencies?" I say.

"Mm, yes. Ada told you how the SVE-1 virus, Grim Fever,

got out into the public?"

"Yeah, her lab assistant was accidentally infected and spread it to a few people, including me."

"Infected, but not by accident."

A cold lump forms in my chest like an ice cube lodged in my esophagus. "What do you mean? He spread it on purpose?"

"No. He was the arrow, not the archer."

"Are you saying someone intentionally infected him and sent him out into public?"

Choi slides a phone from her coat pocket. "Watch this."

A video taken from a phone propped on a table shows a young Asian man with glasses working alongside Ada. He announces everything he's doing aloud like it's an educational video. "Right," Ada says, encouraging the young man. He's typing on a laptop. She tells him it's too hot and to turn down the temperature. "Okay." He stands up and goes off-screen. Ada cocks her head, watching him, and then her bright blue medical gloves flash across the screen as she sprays something on the laptop keyboard. She hid her hands underneath the table. The young man returns and says he lowered it to sixty-eight. He continues typing—with his bare hands.

"Ada infected this kid?"

Choi nods. "Did she tell you what the virus's original intent was?"

"Something about creating a virus that would kill all other viruses?"

"An omnivirus. Yes."

"So why did Ada infect that lab assistant?"

"She wanted to test the spread capacity. They believed it to be benign, but they wanted to test how contagious their virus was. Once they discovered that it was both dangerously contagious and fatal, they called me in. But they weren't forthright with what happened. I discovered the truth along the way."

"Despicable. They couldn't test that in a lab? They had to let it out into the world?"

"Yes. When I learned that, I halted my original work and investigated the company."

"Is that why I never saw you again in Washington?"

She nods.

"What were you planning on doing with Lindsay?"

"We wanted to interview her to find out how she became infected, and most importantly, how she survived. But she saw through our phony CDC cover. Smart girl."

Lindsay's smiling face flashes in the front of my memory.

"That McNulty guy seemed too aggressive for a simple interview," I say as Lindsay's ghost vanishes from my mind.

Choi exhales through her nostrils. "He was not my choice. Peter Creston insisted he send his personal private security detail with me. McNulty was a loose cannon. He could have killed you and Lindsay with that car stunt. If I'd have known what he was planning, I wouldn't have let him."

I flashback to McNulty ramming his car into mine, crushing the passenger side of my truck.

"It was then," Choi says, "that I realized Mr. Creston's intent. He didn't want to question Lindsay; he wanted to kill her."

"Why? Couldn't she have helped with a vaccine?"

"At that time, Mr. Creston wanted no part in finding a vaccine. He wanted to end any trace of survivors that might link back to his lab. Ada Curry later had the idea to create a vaccine from a survivor's blood."

I attempt to let this barrage of information settle, to make some sense. It's too much all at once. I don't know if I can trust Choi. It doesn't appear that I can trust Ada. I rub my temples and try to make sense of it all.

"Why did Ada bring me here? It wasn't for my protection, was it?"

Choi reaches into Ada's leather bag on the table and pulls out a syringe full of clear liquid. She hands it to me. "I believe she intended to kill you once she had your blood."

I take it. "What is this?"

"I would guess it's a lethal dose of something. You are a loose thread. They need to snip you away."

A wad of emotion lodges itself in my throat. I inspect the syringe, turning it from side to side. I'm shocked when it's not fear that floods my mind but curiosity.

Do I deserve to die? Yes, Peter Creston and Ada Curry sent Grim Fever out into the world, but I helped spread it. I helped cause the worst outbreak since the Black Plague. Shouldn't that warrant the ultimate penalty?

Choi opens her mouth to speak when the front door squeaks open. She reaches behind her back and freezes, her eyes tense and focused.

"Ada," a man's voice booms from the front entry, "is it done?"

28

Choi snatches her handgun from behind her back and aims it at the hallway. She raises a finger to her lips.

The footsteps grow louder. "Ada?"

A gray-haired man in a shiny navy blue suit comes around the corner. He sees me, and his face contorts with confusion. He turns his head to see Choi and flinches.

"Don't move," Choi says.

The man twitches like he's going to run, but he thinks better of it and turns toward Choi, hands raised. "Dr. Choi." A nervous smile curls in the corner of his mouth.

Choi flicks the gun to her right, gesturing for him to move away from the hall.

He complies, clears his throat. "You know I'm not here alone, right? No matter what you do to me, you won't make it out of here alive."

Choi maintains a steady gaze, her gun aimed at his chest.

"Where's Ada?" The man's voice cracks, his false bravado wearing thin. "Did you kill her like you killed McNulty?" He sneers at Choi, then eyes me. "Chad Chaucer. The lone survivor." He shakes his head. "Do you realize how much you've cost me?"

"Do you realize how much you've cost me?" The anger leaps off my tongue. "Your virus ruined my life!"

He rolls his eyes. "If you would have just died like everyone else, we would've had it contained. But no, you ran around the country like a little spark among the brush."

"Please stop talking, Mr. Creston," Choi says, her voice emotionless.

"He's—"

"Enough."

Creston's mouth hangs open, his eyes saddened like a scolded child. It's clear he's not used to anyone else controlling the situation, but he's afraid of Choi.

"You've run out of options, Mr. Creston," Choi says after a silent moment. "The truth is out. Evidence of your involvement is already spreading on the internet. Like a little spark among the brush."

"What evidence?"

"Make the correct choice, and you won't get hurt."

Creston laughs. "You think you've got anything on me? Ada might go down, but she'll never turn on me." He smirks. "You've got nothing, and you know it. By the way, you didn't think I'd come here alone, did you?"

From my peripheral view, I catch a shadow moving in the kitchen window.

"Behind you!" I shout to Choi.

Bursts of gunfire.

Shattered glass.

Creston lunges for me.

I stand and plunge the syringe into his chest.

More gunshots.

A warm splash of liquid wets my face.

Hot pain roils in my chest like something took a bite out of me.

Creston wobbles, then swings at me. His arm moves like the minute-hand of a clock, slowed by whatever was in the syringe. I take a step back, easily avoiding his loose fist.

Dizzied, I look at Choi. She rises from a crouched position. Her face is a stone sculpture. She pulls open the door, peeks outside, nods once, then turns around.

I collapse back into the chair. My vision narrows. Everything sounds distorted, echoing like I'm in a tunnel.

Creston staggers forward, wobbling. He glares at Choi. "You…you bitch," he slurs. He takes a step toward her.

Choi lowers her gun and takes a step aside, calm as if avoiding the flight path of a butterfly. Creston collapses, his face slams on the corner of the counter, and his head bounces once off the tile floor.

I'm sleepy. I'm falling. No. I'm…floating.

"Mr. Chau—"

29

Beep. What's beeping?

My eyelids flip open. The dim room is a blur, but judging by the starchy sheets and clinical odor, I recognize I'm in a hospital bed. I'm plugged into various machines, and my mouth tastes like I licked the desert.

"Ah, there you go. You're awake." I don't recognize the voice, but she has a thick Pittsburgh accent.

I open my mouth to speak, but it's too dry, and the raspy sound that comes out doesn't sound like words. "Water, please," I'm able to whisper.

A nurse that reminds me of my mom holds a cup of water near my chin and directs the straw to my lips. I suck in the cool liquid, let it glide over my tongue, and swallow slowly. I've never had a more refreshing sip of water in my entire existence.

"How do you feel?" the nurse asks.

"I don't know." I'm not good or bad. Just...here.

"Doctor'll be by in the next fifteen minutes." She writes something on a whiteboard near the door. "Need anything else?"

I shake my head.

She turns and leaves, her blond ponytail wagging behind her head.

I close my eyes and lie back as memories flood in. Ada's house. Choi. Gunshots. Stabbing a man with a syringe. I wonder how long I've been out. My scratchy eyes can't make out what it says on the whiteboard. Someone else walks into the room. Dark hair. Short stature. Female.

"Hello, Mr. Chaucer, how are you doing?"

"Hi, Dr. Choi. I'm okay. I think."

She approaches my bed.

"Wait," I say. "You're not my doctor, are you?"

She laughs, deeper and more throaty than I expect. "No, I'm not your doctor. Did the nurse tell you the full extent of your injuries?"

I shake my head.

"You were shot in the chest. The bullet broke two ribs, went straight through your right lung, and exited below the opposite shoulder blade, missing your heart and spine by the narrowest of margins."

My head tingles, and sickness swirls in my empty stomach. "Shit."

"You've already had two surgeries in the three days you've been here. A full recovery is expected, though you will require quite a bit of healing time."

I turn my head toward Choi. The room wobbles a bit, and I realize I'm under some heavy pain medication. "Who are you?"

She cocks her head to the side, confusion etched on her forehead.

"I mean, who do you work for?"

"Ah. I'm a contractor of sorts. That's all I will say on the matter."

I let her response fill my hazy mind. I want to pursue it, but I let it go. "What's going to happen to me when I get out of here?" Prison. A nice cell near the yard. A beefy roommate.

"That's why I'm here, Chad."

I think that's the first time she's ever called me by my first name.

"I can arrange for your past to be...corrected."

"You mean the prison outbreaks?"

She dips her chin. "Say the word, and it's done. And I have a contact at the CDC who would love to have you visit, but I'll leave that choice to you."

"Why?"

"I'm not sure I understand. Why what?"

"Why would you do that for me?"

"It wasn't your fault. The virus, I mean. You made a difficult—albeit selfish—choice. But one can understand the decisions you made given your options." Her lips curl into a caring smile. "And you saved my life. I did not see Creston's gunman, and he would have killed us both had you not warned me."

"This is a lot to process."

"It is."

"Hey, what happened to Creston?"

Choi sighs through her nose. "The syringe contained a lethal dose of morphine."

"So...Ada was going to kill me."

"Yes."

"And where is she?"

"In a jail cell."

"And you can make a call and wipe away my rotten past?"

"I can if that's what you wish to do."

I'm lucky to be alive despite all the people I've infected.

Killed. I lost my wife, Leanne. The person who knew me better than I know myself. I lost Lindsay, with whom I shared an unbreakable bond. I fell for a con, a death trap, and somehow escaped with my life.

With moisture finally coming to my eyes, I blink away tears and look at Choi. "I've decided what I want to do."

30

My hospital discharge was eighteen months ago. I needed another surgery, and I have trouble breathing at times, but otherwise, the recovery has been smooth. I stayed in Pittsburgh for multiple therapies and became good friends with my physical therapist. We went to the same high school six years apart. We've discovered several mutual acquaintances.

I've visited some old friends. Told some stories I'm sure they don't believe. I also had dinner with Leanne's parents. All this time, I thought they blamed me for her death, but they were more supportive than I could have ever hoped for. I still keep in contact with them. Lindsay's niece plays for the varsity soccer team, and the family invited me to a game. Lacy has grown to be the spitting image of her aunt; it's almost too painful to look at her.

Dr. Choi—I never learned her first name—helped me get in contact with the CDC. Using my blood, they developed a vaccine that received emergency use authorization five months ago, its effects overwhelmingly positive. The country has gone an entire month without a Grim Fever death.

Ada Curry will spend the rest of her life in federal prison. Even more damning evidence than Choi provided came to light, and it was ugly. Had Peter Creston survived, he would've seen the same fate as Ada. As it is, Creston Widmer Pharmaceuticals collapsed and sold its assets to pay for the multitude of class action lawsuits presented against it.

Now I sit and await my future. The room is silent. My chair squeaks with even the slightest movement, bringing me even more attention.

"Please rise for the honorable Dana Hawking. The People versus Chad David Chaucer is now in session."

Whatever judgment comes, I deserve and will wholly accept.

Made in the USA
Las Vegas, NV
18 February 2021

18155278R00132